The Scarred Santa

by

Lee Ann Sontheimer Murphy

The Scarred Santa

Cover Art by *The Wild Rose Press, Inc.*

The Wild Rose Press, Inc.
PO Box 708
Adams Basin, NY 14410-0708
Visit us at www.thewildrosepress.com

Publishing History
First Edition, 2023
Trade Paperback ISBN 978-1-5092-5079-0
Digital ISBN 978-1-5092-5078-3

Previously Published: Clean Reads, November 2016
Published in the United States of America

Rafe longed for the kind of camaraderie he'd had with the Marines in his unit. They had been friends, brothers, and more. He loved Mike and Gabe, but neither had served in the military, let alone spent years in a war zone. Neither came close to dying and endured a long struggle to survive. They had supported him, though, both flying huge distances to be with him in the hospital, to be there when he endured yet another surgery, and to give support when he faced recovery. They couldn't be with him all the time, but they had come to him as often as they could. So had his mom.

In the silence of the night, with nothing but his thoughts and the falling rain for company, Rafe owned up to what he wanted most of all. He dreamed about finding a woman who could see beyond his ruined face, overlook his scars, and wouldn't be frightened away by his PTSD. His battered heart ached to give love and to be loved. In his various jobs, sometimes he caught a whiff of some sweet perfume, saw a glimpse of a woman's smile, or watched couples holding hands and envied them. He craved such affection, and he hungered for the things he had sacrificed along with his old face—a wife, a home, and kids. A family.

When he withdrew from his circle of relatives, with his physical damage and his issues, those were things Rafe figured he could never have.

But he wanted them just the same.

Dedication

To my late mother, Carol Sontheimer, who first read to me and who always encouraged me to write my own stories.

Chapter One

He hated his first name, now more than ever. Consequently, when his brother Mike—short for Michael, after the Archangel—pounded on the door of his two-room apartment and shouted his full name, Rafe ignored him.

"Raphael Sean Sullivan, open the door before I bust it down."

"You wouldn't." But Rafe knew Mike probably would. He had an Irish temper, quick to flare and slow to burn. So, Rafe opened the door and faced his older brother whose dark hair sported a few strands of gray. "I told you I'm not coming over for Thanksgiving. It's not even November yet."

Mike sighed. "It's not about Thanksgiving, although I still wish you'd join us. It's not like you need to go over the river and through the woods or even around the interstate. All you have to do is walk across the yard and through the back door. Mom won't expect you to bring a covered dish or a store-bought pie or anything. And you get a free turkey dinner with all the trimmings, plus hours with four generations of relatives."

Once Rafe would have loved the holiday and been glad to be part of it all. But that was then, and he was a different man now, changed forever. "If I came to dinner, I'd upset everyone. They would stare and whisper behind my back. Everyone would be too nice and pity me. Last time I joined the family for a holiday, Gramma cried."

"She cried because she was glad to see you, not because she was upset."

"I doubt it. And Gabe's kid screamed and hid because she thought I was a monster."

Mike flopped on the rump-sprung couch. "Deirdre was three. It doesn't mean anything."

Rafe sat in the recliner. "It would if you were the one who resembled Frankenstein's creation or Freddy Krueger," he stated in a quiet tone.

Mike frowned hard. "Don't exaggerate, Rafe. The scars aren't so bad."

"To me, they are." Rafe avoided mirrors as much as possible. The small one attached to the medicine cabinet above the sink remained, but he shaved by touch, not sight. The moment he forgot how acute the damage had been to his face, all it took was one glance to serve as a reminder. His right ear would never be more than a misshapen blob of flesh, but he could hear out of it. The right side of his mouth would always droop a little, and the network of fine scars crisscrossing his cheek would remain. Although his hair had grown back on the right side, the ridged scars from his burns ranged from above his ear to his sternum. Burn scarring covered his right arm from shoulder to his hand, but he covered it with long sleeves. The flesh around his right eye would always be puckered, but Rafe's vision remained intact. His right leg was held together with a titanium rod, but he seldom limped. He didn't mind the leg much because it worked, and any scars there didn't show. His face, however, had suffered too much damage to hide.

Mike's face held anger, not pity. A frown twisted his lips and gave him a harsh appearance as he stared at Rafe. "Forget about Thanksgiving for now. It's not until next month. You'll come or you won't. The reason I came over is to see why you haven't been going to work. There's a lot of flu and crud going around. Are you sick?"

Rafe shook his head. "No, I'm as good as I get. I quit, Mike."

"Again?" Mike's volume increased. "What happened this time?"

With slow steps, Rafe walked over to the window overlooking the back yard. He had worked for the last two months, almost a record for him these days, as an overnight stock clerk at a large discount store. The hours meant fewer people saw his face, and he had almost got to like graveyard shift. When the Halloween merchandise—everything from plastic pumpkins to graphic rubber masks—arrived, Rafe had steeled himself for comments, but none came.

But a few days ago, he'd heard two younger stockers laughing about him. "Some of the kids I worked with said my face was uglier than any mask in the store," he said. "They suggested I could make a lot of money moonlighting at the haunted house and compared my ugly mug to the late-night horror show. Then one of them tried to grab the nub, what's left of my ear, to see if it was latex or what. You know, same old thing, but different day." He steeled himself for Mike to chastise him again.

"I'm sorry, man. You shouldn't have to put up with such nonsense. Your coworkers must have been immature." Mike's voice softened with a gentler tone.

"First-year students at the community college," Rafe said. "At their age, I was already a Marine."

"I know." Mike's face shifted as he looked away from Rafe. He twisted his fingers together, an old indication the conversation made him uncomfortable.

"And I'd still be one if…" Rafe had to stop. If he kept talking, he might cry, and he refused to cry in front of his big brother.

"If you hadn't got injured in Helmand Province," Mike interjected, finishing his sentence. "Brother, I know, and I wish you were still a jarhead. But you're not. You've been home almost two years, and you've had more jobs than I can count. We worry about you."

We meant Mike and his wife, Charlotte. It also meant the whole family and included their brother, Gabe, and his bride, Amber, and their widowed mother. It included a large family circle made up of his maternal grandmother, several aunts, and uncles, and too many cousins. "I wish you wouldn't." Rafe spoke in an even tone.

"We can't help it. We're family. You can't hide out in the garage apartment for the rest of your life. You need to keep a job and build a life. Have you thought any more about what you might like to do, job-wise?"

He had and thinking made his situation worse. "All I know how to do is to be a Marine." Rafe stared through the window without really seeing what was outside. "There aren't a lot of jobs in the civilian sector for those skills, especially not for someone who looks like me." To emphasize his point, Rafe faced his brother so Mike could get the full, gory effect.

But Mike didn't even blink. "So, retrain. Take

some classes at the community college and get a degree. You're smart, Rafe. There are so many careers you could do if you just would. A lot of people with a military background go into law enforcement."

Once, Rafe had considered the field. But now he couldn't imagine life as a police officer or deputy. He snorted. "If I did, my resume might sound impressive. But if I get an interview, the first look at me would be enough to change their mind."

"I don't agree, but I'm not going to fight with you." Mike rose and crossed the room to lay a hand on Rafe's shoulder. "Have you thought about anything else?"

"I've managed to rule out overnight stocker." Rafe could almost taste the bitterness of his words. "Same goes for telemarketing, night security guard, loading trucks, working for a florist and making deliveries, janitor in a residential care facility, dishwasher, line cook, and running a road grader."

"I'm sure the right job for you is waiting, Rafe."

He shrugged. "If it's true, I don't know what it might be or where to find it. Maybe you should find a job for me, Mike. Do you think I'd do a great job selling insurance in your office?"

Mike's face flushed red.

For once, Rafe managed to get a reaction.

"You would, if you'd put your mind to it and not be so focused on your scars."

Rafe laughed but not with mirth. The sound had the hollow edge of dry bones rattling in a cold wind. "It's easy to say so when people don't gasp with horror in the supermarket, and when your nephew doesn't offer you a plastic toy ear because he noticed you're lacking one."

"Matthew wanted to help," Mike said, speaking about his son. "He's six, remember. Maybe you don't since you didn't come to his birthday party."

"I know how old the kid is," Rafe wanted the conversation to end and sighed. "Isn't it about time for Charlotte to put supper on the table?"

"Almost. Would you like to join us? It's beef stew and biscuits."

For a moment, the idea of warm stew with tender meat and rich gravy populated with a few vegetables tempted Rafe. A flaky, buttered biscuit would taste so good. He opened his mouth to say 'yes,' then imagined Mike's family gazing everywhere but at him. Whenever he was around, their conversation muted, and everyone stared at their plates. "Thanks, but I'll pass."

"Mom would love it if you'd come."

Mike and his brood shared the rambling two-story house where the Sullivan brothers had grown up with their widowed mother. When Rafe did show up, Mom tried her best to treat him the way she always had but failed. She chattered too much about her sewing, knitting, and ladies church group. She never trekked across the back yard to visit his apartment, and he thought he made her uncomfortable. "Maybe another time," he said, although they both knew he probably wouldn't accept other invitations.

Mike stood. "I don't suppose you'd want to go deer hunting with me when the season opens."

Once, Rafe had loved the male bonding, the autumn woods still bright with color, the crisp air, and the chance to bring home venison. Now, with some serious PTSD issues, he worried the blast of a shotgun might trigger an episode, and if it didn't, the scent of blood would make him sick. He'd seen far too much of it, and the slightest hint of its coppery smell brought him back to Afghanistan, a place he would rather not visit even in memory. Rafe shook his head. "No, Mike."

"All right, Rafe. You need to get out more, hang out with friends, and meet some new people. And you know, I have an idea about a job. I'll check into it and get back with you. Is there anything I can get you before I go home?"

"No, but Mike?"

"Yeah?"

"Thanks. I know you're trying to help."

Mike crossed the space between them and gave him a bear hug. Rafe avoided being touched most of the time, but right now, the contact and the emotion behind it warmed some cold, dark place within. He let himself hug Mike back before stepping away. The moment his brother exited the door, Rafe shut it. He didn't want Mike to notice the tears in his eyes.

As Rafe ate a cold bologna sandwich, he thought about the beef stew he might have had with some regret. Part of him ached to enjoy a meal with his family, with Mike's three kids laughing and sharing about their school day, with his mother smiling at them, and with Charlotte talking about some little incident at work. Mike used to have funny little stories about his insurance office or about clients.

Growing up, their family meals had always been time for talking, and Rafe missed the connection more than he would ever admit to Mike. After his solitary supper, Rafe curled up in bed with a book. Since coming home after three tours in Iraq and two in Afghanistan, he watched little television. Before, he'd been into action movies with plenty of explosions and gunfire and violence, but after he had lived through it, his taste changed.

So, he listened to music, everything from classic rock and country to traditional Irish music or read. He fed his e-reader a steady supply of novels he checked out through the local library online and sometimes bought a few. In his search for something different, Rafe had discovered Dickens and read everything from *Oliver Twist* to *David Copperfield.* He enjoyed mysteries more than he could have imagined. And although he wouldn't admit it to anyone, especially not his brothers, he liked a few romance novels. They were his guilty secret.

Sleep came hard for Rafe, so he read far into the night. A heavy downpour pattered on the roof, and he put aside his device to listen. He rose and padded across the linoleum floor to the window. Beneath his fingertips, the cool glass contrasted with his body heat. Rafe considered getting dressed and grabbing a jacket to walk in the rain. He could without drawing curious stares but decided against it. With his luck, Mike would be peering outside and see him. And his brother would hustle outside to offer advice and support. *He means well, but he doesn't understand.*

Long past midnight, Rafe prowled his small space like a caged animal or a prisoner in a cell. Since he wasn't working, nights brought out restlessness. His brother's visit made him think about things he tried to ignore. More than anything, he wanted to find somewhere he fit and could build a life. He would like nothing better than to hang out with friends, dine out, go to a movie or a concert, or work on somebody's car. Rafe wished he had the courage to attend church more often, but the sympathy, the sidelong glances, and the whispers were too much to bear. He would enjoy singing in the choir, belting out familiar hymns and learning new music, but he knew he'd never handle the scrutiny. If only, he thought, people would judge him by what he was within, not by his grotesque appearance, then he might overcome his issues.

Rafe longed for the kind of camaraderie he'd had with the Marines in his unit. They had been friends, brothers, and more. He loved Mike and Gabe, but neither had served in the military, let alone spent years in a war zone. Neither came close to dying and endured a long struggle to survive. They had supported him, though, both flying huge distances to be with him in the hospital, to be there when he endured yet another surgery, and to give support when he faced recovery. They couldn't be with him all the time, but they had come to him as often as they could. So had his mom.

In the silence of the night, with nothing but his thoughts and the falling rain for company, Rafe owned up to what he wanted most of all. He dreamed about finding a woman who could see beyond his ruined face, overlook his scars, and wouldn't be frightened away by his PTSD. His battered heart ached to give love and to be loved. In his various jobs, sometimes he caught a whiff of some sweet perfume, saw a glimpse of a woman's smile, or watched couples holding hands and envied them. He craved such affection, and he hungered for the things he had sacrificed along with his old face—a wife, a home, and kids. A family.

When he withdrew from his circle of relatives, with his physical damage and his issues, those were things Rafe figured he could never have.

But he wanted them just the same.

Chapter Two

For two days, Rafe did nothing and didn't leave the apartment. He spent long hours in bed, dozing during the day to make up for his nighttime insomnia. Although the crisp, cooler temperatures of October had once appealed, he did his best to ignore the weather. On Saturday, he heard Mike's kids, six-year-old Matthew and eight-year-old Catherine, in the backyard.

The kids ran through the fallen leaves, whooping aloud with delight.

Their antics made Rafe smile. He remembered doing the same.

Ten minutes later, Mike showed up. "Come rake leaves with us, bro."

Rafe almost rejected the offer from habit, but the gorgeous weather tempted him. He craved fresh air and time outside. The backyard lay between the house and freestanding garage. One side overlooked the yard, and the other the alley behind. On the north side, the adjacent house sat higher, and he doubted the older couple living there would be outside. To the south, a high hedge blocked the view from the neighbor. He wouldn't be on display. "All right, Mike, sure." His brother's grin pleased him. Rafe had done little to make Mike smile since his return almost two years ago.

"Good. Grab a jacket and come down."

He wore a knitted hat, too, pulled down low

enough to hide his missing ear.

The kids greeted him with exuberant shouts and hugged him.

Their affection touched him, and his heart brimmed full with emotion. He loved those kids and their display made him happy. Rafe mussed Matthew's hair and tugged Catherine's braid. "Let's get to work." Raking in the sunshine proved to be a pleasant task. As he worked, Rafe kept the intact left side of his face visible from the house. This way, if his mom decided to watch, she could pretend nothing had happened to her youngest son, the one she'd always found good looking.

She had named her sons after the archangels Michael, Gabriel, and Raphael. Since Rafe came last, he got saddled with the fanciest name. He'd never much cared for it, but after his injuries, he loathed it. Everyone had always considered the Sullivan brothers good-looking, Rafe most of all, so his brothers had always teased him about his looks. They'd even nicknamed him "Angel Face," but his dad shut that down with speed.

After the explosion and the damage, Rafe figured no one would compare his face to an angel's. The bad side suggested devils. The one time he'd tried to joke Mom should have named him Lucifer instead of Raphael, he'd made his mother cry and his brothers angry. He meant it to be funny, but in his bitterness, he'd missed the mark.

For the first time in longer than he could recall, he forgot about his scars and injuries as he worked. The October sun on his back was soothing, and he appreciated the warmth. The task gave him focus, and by noon, he, Mike, and the children had raked the leaves into a huge pile. "Are we going to bag them up or what?" Rafe asked, leaning on the rake.

Mike shook his head. "Naw, I thought we'd burn them after I let the kids jump into the leaves. We'll probably have to rake them back up first, but they'll enjoy it."

Rafe chuckled. "Yeah, we always did."

Running through the autumn leaves, Matthew and Catherine squealed and shouted. They rolled in them and scattered armfuls with delight. When the fun came to an end, the kids headed inside.

The brothers raked everything back into one huge pile.

"We'll burn it after lunch," Mike said.

On cue, with perfect timing, Mom came outside. "Come on and let's eat," she called. "We're having chili dogs with macaroni and cheese."

Rafe leaned his rake against the fence. The illusion of normalcy faded. He figured he could slip up to his apartment, eat a sandwich, and maybe return. Or maybe not. He took one step in the general direction of the garage, but Mike stopped him.

"Don't take off," he pleaded, his voice low. "Come have lunch. If you don't, Mom's going to be upset."

"I don't want her to be," Rafe said. "But, Mike, I'd rather…"

"You'd rather run away. I know. But if you do, she'll cry. It'll put a damper on the fun the kids have had. It won't do much for me or Charlotte, either. None of us care about your scars or how you look."

"I do." Every time Rafe thought about the face he now wore, it made his stomach ache. He couldn't get past the idea he resembled some creature from a horror

13

film and had trouble accepting his appearance wouldn't ever change.

"Yeah, I get it. Come on, Rafe. I know you had a good morning. Don't ruin it."

Rafe glanced at his mother, trying to think up a plausible reason why he wouldn't join them. Mom glanced at him with a bright smile so he couldn't bear to let her down. Since his dad died in a traffic accident while he was in Afghanistan, before Rafe was injured, Anne Sullivan had struggled to cope. According to Mike and Gabe, the news he'd been seriously hurt and evacuated to Landstuhl Regional Medical Center in Germany had hit her hard, almost destroyed her after the loss of her husband. She hadn't flown to his bedside, but Mike had, even though at the time Rafe hadn't appreciated it. "All right," he mumbled. "I'll have lunch, but I swear to God, if there's any talk of monsters or ugly creatures I'm outta there."

Mike glared. "There won't be. The kids love you, you know?"

He did, and he adored them. Rafe got a kick out of their childish enthusiasm for everything. Gabe's kids were equally great. Nieces and nephews were the closest he'd ever have to kids of his own. It grieved him more than he would admit to anyone. "Yeah, let's go eat."

He expected to eat in the kitchen, but with six, it would have been tight, so they put together their plates in there and carried them to the dining room. When the family paused to say grace, Rafe bowed his head after an awkward moment. The old habit was one he'd lost in recent years, but somehow, with his mom's soft voice asking the blessing, it seemed right.

After his diet of cold sandwiches, canned tamales, and frozen pizza, the chili dogs tasted fantastic. His mom's special chili sauce complimented the wieners, and he ate two along with a heaping portion of mac and cheese. Conversation flowed easily between them.

The kids chatted about school, last night's high school football game, and raking leaves.

Charlotte, a substitute teacher, shared a story about subbing high school history and how one of the students had asked her if she had been a kid during World War II. "Some of them have no sense of time," she said with a laugh.

No one asked Rafe about work so he figured Mike must have told them he had quit.

After lunch, Mike glanced at Rafe with the box of matches in one hand. "Is the fire going to bother you?"

Rafe sometimes liked the way his family could be solicitous, but there were times when he hated it. "Probably not," he answered. Right now, he appreciated the concern. "Controlled small fires like burning leaves or a barbecue grill or something isn't a problem. I might freak out with something big and out of control. Like they say, don't play with fire, you might get burned. I was, so I have a lot of fear and respect for it."

"Are you sure?" Mike raised his eyebrows, skeptical.

"Yeah, Mike, and thanks for asking first." Rafe stayed while Mike burned the leaves and sat in a lawn chair under the maple tree while the fire died down to ashes.

Charlotte rounded up the kids for Matthew's soccer match, but Mike stayed home and so did their mom.

She brought them snickerdoodle cookies fresh out

of the oven, a favorite treat since childhood.

"These are good, Mom," he told her. "Thanks for making cookies." Her gesture touched him.

She laughed. "You're welcome, Rafe, but I didn't bake just for you. The annual harvest dinner and bake sale is tomorrow at church. I made snickerdoodles, peanut butter cookies, and brownies. Charlotte made Aunt Hattie's cherry cake. You should come. The dinner menu is barbecued brisket and baked ham with scalloped potatoes, green beans, and corn. I think Susan Collins is making her famous hot rolls, too."

He could almost taste the food, tender smoked meat and ham basted with a pineapple glaze. In high school, the harvest dinner had been a favorite. He'd managed to attend once while home on leave, but since his return to civilian life, Rafe had avoided public events. "Aw, Mom…"

She patted his shoulder. "It's wonderful to see you get out of the house, son. I'm enjoying talking with you. I miss you, but you know that."

Uncomfortable, Rafe squirmed in the chair. "I just live across the back yard, Mom."

"I know, but I see so little of you. It would be wonderful to have you join us at church."

The simple statement stung. She asked little of him and had respected his desire for privacy. Since he'd moved above the garage, she hadn't visited once he'd settled. But she'd provided dishes and pans for the kitchen, linens for the bed, and most of the furniture. The bulk was hand-me-downs, but still, she hadn't had to give him anything. He hated to do anything to hurt her feelings. "I don't know. I'll think about it." Rafe didn't really mean it, so her answering smile evoked some guilt.

She kissed his forehead and returned to the house.

Until now, he and Mike had talked about safe subjects—old times, football, and the weather—but silence dropped between them like a rock wall.

After a few minutes, Mike rose and poked the dying fire with the rake. "You should cut her some slack, Rafe. Today's been a good day, but she hasn't been feeling well, and she has a doctor's appointment on Monday."

Concern cut through his perennial self-pity and preservation. "What's wrong with Mom?"

Mike shrugged. "She's been having a lot of headaches, some of them pretty bad."

"Is it serious? Is she okay?"

"I don't know. It's why she made the appointment to find out. It's good to know you still care."

"Of course, I do. I care about her and all of you." Rafe's shoulders drooped. His brother's sarcasm stung. He really thought they should realize he loved them all, very much.

"Then maybe you could take her to the doctor since you're not working. Otherwise, one of us will have to take time off. I can't—I've got my regional manager coming in for a meeting on Tuesday."

He would rather face down an angry rattlesnake than go anywhere near a medical center. Twenty surgeries, too much hospital time, and too many appointments had given him an aversion to anything similar. But this involved *his mother.* Rafe sighed, hard. "All right, I'll take her. And I'll go to church with you all tomorrow and stay for the dinner."

Mike's face lit up with a smile. "Thanks, bro. I

appreciate it, and I know Mom will, too. It's good for you to get out among the living."

The living. The phrase stuck in Rafe's consciousness and haunted him. He had survived traumatic injuries. Many of his comrades hadn't. Mike's words brought home to him how much he had retreated from life, something he never intended to do. And he hadn't understood how much he had until now.

On Sunday morning, he put on dress clothes for the first time since he'd worn Marine blues. Rafe had to borrow a white dress shirt, a red tie, and a navy suit jacket from Mike's closet. He wore them with his best jeans, unwilling to wear slacks. The clothes were odd and unfamiliar, but when he chanced a glance in the mirror, he appeared dapper, if his gaze didn't focus on his ruined right side.

At church he planned to slip into a back pew, as much out of sight as possible, but when they entered the sanctuary, Mom put her arm through his. Rafe walked her down the aisle to her usual seat, about three rows from the front. Self-conscious, he bowed his head and hoped people might think he was deep in prayer. He would rather not talk, but several people gathered around to greet him.

"It's so nice to see you in church." Marjorie Carmichael, one of Mom's church friends, offered a compliment. "You look so nice in a sport jacket."

Nice? Rafe wouldn't have chosen the word, but he thanked her. And he listened as a steady stream of church members asked about his mom's health. As he expected, she downplayed her recent headaches and changed the subject each time it came up. Rafe gathered she had missed a few of her ladies' group meetings and even church because of her headaches—something he hadn't known, even though he lived on the same property.

The service began with music and the first song, "On Eagles' Wings," had always been one of his favorites. He sang along, letting his voice soar and blend with the others. A few more hymns followed, and by the time the congregation settled down for the sermon, Rafe experienced calm. For the moment, he forgot to see if anyone stared, caught up in the music and the powerful joy it brought.

The pastor, Eric Wynn, had been serving their church for a long time, even before Rafe joined the Marines. His message failed to keep Rafe's attention the way the songs had, and he watched others. Some listened with complete interest, but many didn't. A few had cell phones out. Whether they were texting or playing games or checking the weather, none of it sat well with Rafe. Not at church, because this wasn't the time or place for such.

In the rear, where he had wanted to sit, he noticed Elmer Gardner, one of the oldest members of the church. He had to be well into his nineties by now, because he'd fought in World War II. Elmer had seen action, too, including the landing at Anzio in Italy and the fight for Monte Cassino. The old man sat in a wheelchair, but he appeared cognizant of everything around him. Rafe recalled he'd offered a blessing when he left for boot camp and later, he'd overheard his parents discussing how sensitive Elmer was about his scars. "What scars?" Rafe had asked because he had never noticed.

His dad shook his head. "Don't tell me you've

never seen them. He suffered some extensive burns in the war. He's not bald— he shaves his head because hair won't grow over some of the scar ridges. I'll have to tell him you never paid any attention to them, because he's always so sure people are staring."

Rafe hadn't thought about the moment in years and not since his own injuries. From this distance, he couldn't see Elmer's scars, but he would make a point to speak to him after the service. "I want to say hello to Elmer."

As soon as the last song ended, Rafe dashed out of the pew. He approached the old man who offered him a huge smile.

"Rafe Sullivan! How are you, son?" The veteran extended his hand.

Rafe shook it. "I'm all right. It's good to see you here."

"Same about you, young man," Elmer said. "I'm glad you made it home, after all."

The simple statement meant so much from another combat veteran. Rafe nodded. Up close, Elmer's scars were visible on scrutiny, but they weren't the first thing anyone would notice. A few raised, rough patches could be seen on his head with a larger section behind Elmer's left ear. If they had once been red, they must have faded over time. *Great. Maybe in sixty or seventy years mine won't be so obvious. But I'll never grow another ear.*

A strong desire to bolt struck him, and he might have run, if so many people hadn't surrounded him. Rafe shook hands, accepted hugs, and made small talk as he worked his way through the crowd.

His mom, the center of her own circle, stood to one

side.

So he headed for her.

"There you are." She linked her arm through his. "Are you handling the attention you're getting? I know it's a huge change from your usual isolation. If it's too much, we can go home."

He had been ready to leave, but now, for his mother's sake, Rafe wanted to stay. "It's a little intense, but I'm okay."

"Then let's go downstairs. The harvest dinner is in the fellowship hall."

No wonder he'd been inhaling some delicious aromas during the service. They descended the stairs where Mike's family joined them. Across the room, Rafe spotted Gabe, Amber, and their three children. The long rows of tables he remembered had been replaced with large round ones, each seating twelve or more. With any luck, one would hold all the Sullivans with no room for anyone else.

Everyone milled around until the pastor asked for quiet and said a blessing. Then they swarmed the tables of food, Rafe among them.

He sat with his back to most of the room, facing his family. Matthew and his cousin, Eamon, flanked Rafe. The food tasted marvelous, but Rafe became more than a little ill at ease. Multiple conversations filled the air with sound, and the hall seemed overly warm. He focused on his food— the brisket was amazing, so tender and with such a rich, smoke taste— and tried not to freak.

His nephew, Matthew, leaned close, put one small hand on Rafe's arm, and whispered, "Don't worry, Uncle Rafe. I've got your six."

The familiar phrase, meaning so much, almost broke Rafe down into tears. His young nephew's perception touched him, too. "Thanks, kid. Then I know I'm good."

Matthew rewarded him with a gap-toothed grin.

Rafe's appetite returned, and he enjoyed the meal. After two of his mom's snickerdoodle cookies—he would never pass up those for any other dessert—he wondered if he wanted a cup of coffee enough to face the crowd. As he debated, he saw her and forgot all about coffee.

Her dark, shiny hair fell midway down her back, and she was laughing, her heart-shaped face glowing with mirth. Her dark-brown eyes reminded Rafe of his favorite chocolate pudding. He watched with interest as she giggled, her petite nose wrinkled. It tilted up slightly at the end. Her generous mouth curved into a smile, and her cheeks flushed pink. She noticed his attention but didn't look away.

She's the prettiest thing I've seen in forever, and she didn't flinch when she saw me.

He leaned across his nephew to his mother. "Mom, do you know her name?"

"Whose name?"

Pointing would be rude so he didn't. "I'm talking about the young lady, the brunette with the apron over the red dress. The one at the dessert table."

"Her name is Sheena Dunmore.

"Do you know her?" He wondered if he did. Rafe doubted he could have forgotten someone so lovely.

"She's Mrs. Gallagher's granddaughter," his mother said. "She isn't from here, but she's lived here for several years. Why?"

Rafe schooled his voice to be casual. "I just wondered."

Across the table his brothers exchanged glances, but neither one mentioned anything about his question. Rafe hoped they didn't. He didn't need their good-natured teasing about a girl.

He kept his gaze on Sheena until the end of the dinner, and she remained in his thoughts for the rest of the afternoon.

Chapter Three

On Monday, Rafe drove his mother to her doctor's appointment. The yellow brick clinic downtown was familiar. In their childhood, every time one of the boys had a sore throat, ran a fever, or had a bellyache, Mom had brought them here to see Dr. Sheldon. His name was no longer listed on the sign in front, but when they entered, the narrow hallway hadn't changed at all. The place smelled the same, too, an antiseptic aroma tempered with some floral air freshener.

"Who's your doctor?" Rafe asked as they sat in a pair of hard plastic chairs.

"Dr. Perry. Dr. Sheldon retired years ago if you were wondering."

Despite her calm expression, the way his mother bounced one knee reminded him she had to be anxious about this. Her appointment was at eight thirty. They were still waiting at nine.

As the waiting room filled, Rafe did his best to ignore any curious glances. He didn't know if there were any because he kept his head down, reading an ancient copy of *Field and Stream*. Because she expected it, Rafe accompanied his mother back to the small exam room, where a nurse took her vitals and recorded them.

Dr. Perry consulted them. "Tell me about your headaches."

"Oh, I have them several times a week these days. Some are worse than others."

"On a scale of one to ten, how would you rate the pain?"

Mom tilted her head to consider her answer. "I guess I would say seven or eight."

Her reply startled Rafe and gave him a moment of guilt. He'd never realized her headaches were that intense or painful.

The doctor checked her pupils with a flashlight. "How long do they last and what relieves them?"

"They last anywhere from thirty minutes to a few hours," his mother replied. "I usually take a couple of aspirins, but the only thing I've found to help is taking a break and resting my eyes. I sometimes lie down for awhile and close them. A cold pack helps, too."

Her admission startled Rafe. He'd failed to realize how severe his mother's headaches had become, and he should have. Shame that he focused too much on his own issues and not his family's rose in his gut.

"Do you do a lot of reading or needlework?"

"Both."

"Have you ever worn any type of glasses? Even over-the-counter reading glasses?"

Anne Sullivan shook her head. "No, I haven't. Why?"

The way that the doctor smiled and patted his mom's hand reassured Rafe. "I think you might need glasses. Your vitals are good, your blood pressure is well within normal limits, and overall, you appear to be healthy. I could order a battery of tests, do some scans, but I like to keep things simple—and inexpensive—if possible. I'd recommend you have an eye exam and see if you might need to be fitted with prescription glasses. If so, and the headaches go away, I'd say we found the reason. If they continue or you don't need any visual aids, then we'll look farther. What do you think?"

"Sounds reasonable."

Rafe exhaled a long sigh of relief. He'd been more worried than he wanted anyone to know.

On the way to the car, Mom told him, "It probably sounds silly, but I hope I do need glasses. I've been so worried that I might have something terrible wrong with me."

"I guess you need to make an appointment with an optometrist." He wanted to head home and retreat to his quiet apartment. Rafe had enjoyed church and the harvest dinner far more than he had expected, but he craved some solitary space.

"Oh, let's go the mall. They have one of those eyeglass places with an optometrist on duty, and sometimes you can get your glasses in an hour. It would be the easiest, if it's all right with you, Rafe."

It wasn't, but he faked it. "Sure, Mom, if it's what you want." Since his recovery and homecoming, Rafe hadn't set foot into a mall. In his teen years, he'd been fond of the video arcade and hanging out with friends, but once he joined the Marine Corps, his interest in malls waned. He avoided department stores because of the multiple mirrors, and he shopped online as much as possible.

The optical shop proved to be a major nightmare. Racks and racks of eyeglass frames were all backed with mirrored glass. More mirrors where prospective buyers could model the frames were between the displays. Round mirrors at each consulting table provided more reflections. Bright lighting focused on the displays, and Rafe cringed. Dread tightened his chest, and nausea threatened to turn his stomach inside out. He clutched his hands into taut fists. "Mom." He spit out the word with urgency.

She came to a halt, eyes wide. "What's wrong, Rafe?"

"I can't handle all the mirrors. If it's okay, I'll wait for you outside." His lungs must not be working, because he had to work to breathe. Rafe perspired, and his palms became wet. Anxiety clawed through his nervous system with the wild bite of a beast. He needed a quick infusion of fresh air and a little space. Otherwise, he would freak out or faint or embarrass them both.

"It's fine," Anne Sullivan said. She wore a concerned expression. "I can do this some other time, if you need to leave."

He pulled himself together for her sake. "No, I want you to get your eyes checked and get some glasses. Call me when you're done. I'll be in the mall. I'm good, or I will be as soon as I get away from the mirrors. If you don't see me when you're finished, just call me. I might walk the mall a little."

"Are you sure?" Her smile had wilted into a frown.

He knew that was his fault. He did his best to act casual and less panicked. Rafe leaned over and kissed her cheek. "I am, one hundred percent. Take your time."

"All right, then. I'll see you after while." Mom kissed his forehead, which had probably left a lipstick smear. If he didn't hate mirrors, he would find one to see but right now he didn't care if she had.

Heart racing, Rafe hurried out of the store and into the mall. He resisted the urge to run, but he searched for the closest exit. Once he had some air and calmed down, he would require something cold, sweet, and caffeinated. A bench loomed just outside one of the side entrances, and he made for it on wobbling legs. When he reached it, Rafe all but collapsed onto it and gasped in the cool October air. After several deep breaths, he shuddered hard, put his head in his hands, and willed the moment to pass. He stopped shaking and thought he might be able to sit upright.

Someone tapped his back. "Are you all right?"

The voice was soft and feminine, the tone kind and questioning. "I will be," he said. "Give me a minute." Rafe raised his head and saw her. He froze and wondered if he could fake a faint. Embarrassment sent heat blasting through him. The woman who sat beside him, her hand resting on his back and her face furrowed was Sheena Dunmore. Up close, he found her even prettier than at he had at church, but he wanted to sink out of sight into the concrete at his feet.

"Hey, what's the matter?" A worry line divided her forehead.

Rafe failed to think of words to explain that he freaked out because his PTSD, never distant, had flared.

"Tell me what you need. Talk to me." Sheena's voice became lower but urgent. "Do I need to call someone or an ambulance? Dig through your pockets to find some meds or what?"

If he didn't answer, she probably would do something he would regret. "No, I'm okay. I just got a little worked up over nothing. I'm good, now." Babbling made him appear unstable, and he knew it.

The fact she sat on his left bothered Rafe, too. He figured she hadn't noticed the ruined side of his face. When she didn't respond, he expected her to go away, but instead she took his hand.

She fingered the stainless steel Marine Corps ring he always wore. "I'd say you had a PTSD episode. Something triggered you."

"Yeah." Rafe swallowed around a lump in his throat then cleared it. His voice emerged as a rough whisper. "I'm sorry."

"You don't need to be sorry." Her gaze met his, and she stroked the back of his hand.

Rafe wished she would leave before she saw the physical damage. She must already be aware of the emotional baggage. "I don't want to keep you from shopping."

"You're not. I think I saw you yesterday, at a church dinner?"

He surrendered any hope she hadn't noticed his scars or that she didn't know who he was. "You did."

"You're one of the Sullivan brothers, aren't you?"

Rafe sighed. "I'm the youngest."

"I'm Sheena Dunmore. Your mom knows my grandma."

He dredged up the name his mom had given him yesterday. "Mrs. Gallagher."

"Yes. So, what's your name? I'm sorry I don't know."

"Rafe," he said. "How did you realize I had an episode?"

"You mean how did I recognize PTSD?"

He nodded.

"My dad was an army sergeant. Both of my

grandfathers are veterans, and my brother, Jamie, is still in the service. Two of my cousins were in the Middle East—one in Iraq, one in Afghanistan. Are you okay now?"

"Yeah, I'm good." When she narrowed her eyes and studied his face, he added, "I really am, thanks."

"If you're sure, all right." Sheena released his hand. "Are you alone?"

"Mom's getting glasses at the optical place." He must sound like an utter dork.

Sheena shook her head. "Okay. Well, I'm about to grab some lunch before my break is over. Would you like to join me?"

If he ate right now, he'd be sick. "I could use a cold drink."

"Then let's go to the food court and get something before I have to be back at the bookstore."

His mind had cleared, but he couldn't quite wrap it around the conversation they were having. Rafe hadn't talked to a woman this way since forever, or before the last raid in Helmand Province. "Do you work there?"

Her smile sparkled with more than a little pride. "I'm the manager. Let's go, Rafe, before someone comes looking for me." Sheena stood and offered her hand.

Rafe took it and waited for her to take a long, hard look at his damaged features. He steeled himself for the inevitable gasp, then the expression of pity or horror or both. It didn't happen. Instead, they walked down the mall to the food court.

She ordered a chicken sandwich and fries.

Rafe got a soda, and they sat together at a tiny table tucked in one corner of the noisy, large room. He sipped his drink. The more the caffeine and sugar flooded his senses, the more he improved. Sheena talked to him as if she'd known him forever, about books, about the town, about everything except his scars. She never glanced away, and she met his gaze without blinking.

For those precious moments, he enjoyed a respite from being ugly. Rafe became too caught up in the moment to remember to be self-conscious. For the first time, he enjoyed time spent with a pretty woman. Every detail, from the soft scent of her lavender perfume to the way her hair lay behind her shoulders, pleased him, and he knew he would remember all of it. He almost forgot that he was waiting for his mom, and Rafe considered that he might ask this woman out on a date when it happened.

"Mommy, Mommy, look, it's the monster from the movie. It's Frankenstein! It's the monster." The small child's voice came from another table but with maximum volume.

At the first mention of a monster, Rafe went still. He didn't have to see the chubby little fingers pointing or hear the mother's hushed admonition to be nice. His momentary fairy tale had transformed into a nightmare. The short span of time when he'd been Rafe, the old Rafe, ended, and he required willpower not to bolt. More aware than ever of his damaged face, acutely certain the whispers he heard were about him, he struggled to find words to excuse himself.

Sheena reached across the table and grasped both his hands in hers. "Ignore it, Rafe."

"I can't." His breathing increased until he almost panting, despite the fact Sheena's tone came across as gentle yet firm.

"It doesn't matter what that child said. He doesn't understand, and it doesn't change who you are."

Before he could say more, his cell phone buzzed, and he answered. "Hello."

"Rafe, where are you?"

He drew a breath and tried to calm. "Mom, I'm in the food court. I'll be there in two minutes."

His mother laughed and told him, "Don't bother. I see you.

He shifted his head to see her approaching. A pair of tortoiseshell, horn-rimmed spectacles rested on her nose, and her grin revealed her delight.

"Hello, Mrs. Sullivan," Sheena greeted her. "I like your glasses. They're attractive."

Mom's grin widened. "Thank you! I can see so much more clearly."

Rafe cleared his throat. "They look great, Mom. Are you ready to go?"

A little of her happy look faded. "I am if you are. I thought maybe we could go to lunch somewhere unless you've already eaten."

Hours of being on public display made his stomach clench. Rafe would rather go home and be alone, but he didn't want to disappoint Mom. "No, I just had a cool drink."

"Will you be okay with eating out? I know the mirrors bothered you at the eye place. If it's too much, just tell me, son. I realize the mall is a big change from being holed up in your apartment."

Her perception meant a lot, but he still wanted to please her although he'd rather just go home. "It'll be all right."

"Sheena, would you like to join us?" Mom asked.

"I would, thanks, but I have to get back to the bookstore. I enjoyed talking to you, Rafe."

He wanted to say something witty or memorable, but all he told her was, "Yeah, me, too."

"Maybe I'll see you at church." Sheena picked up her purse, slung it over one shoulder, and paused. Facing him, she lifted one hand and touched his cheek; not the unblemished, smooth one but the one webbed with scars. "Take care, Rafe."

Her touch soothed him and agitated him at the same time. Where her fingers brushed, his skin tingled. Sheena evoked the kind of emotions he thought he'd never have again. He watched her walk through the crowds at the mall, her black hair swinging like a satin curtain, until she passed out of sight. He sighed. "Let's go, Mom."

Anne frowned, but she said nothing.

She didn't ask him about Sheena or any more about what upset him at the optical place.

"I'm thinking about Mexican or Chinese. You pick."

He would rather go home and brood. Rafe needed time to process his day out in the land of the living, alone and at home, but he chose Mexican. He knew his mother wouldn't take no for an answer. That rankled—he wished she wouldn't try to force him into being out in public or use love as a whip hand. They ate cheese enchiladas and refried beans at a place he remembered from before. Then he drove home, making conversation with his mother, and shared her hope her headaches were over.

Rafe retreated to his apartment. He locked the door

and sat in silence, mind brimming and emotions raw. His systems were overloaded. First, Saturday with his family, raking leaves and sharing a meal, had been a lot to absorb for a reclusive man. Then he had managed church, the harvest dinner, survived too much talking, and had been intrigued with his first sight of Sheena.

Today, he'd endured a doctor's visit when he hated all things medical for obvious reasons, freaked out when confronted with a host of mirrors, faced the mall, and had an unexpected encounter with the pretty woman he admired. He'd managed the first social moment he'd had in ages, relaxed his guard, and then he had been hit with the same old careless hurt. All of it piled up, greater than he would have thought he could endure, but even more, Rafe had to deal with Sheena's brief caress.

Her touch, coupled with her apparent acceptance of his scars and other baggage, undid him. Rafe didn't know what to think. His emotions were a wild storm brewing, and so he tried to stall it. He took a long shower, he paced the floor, he put on music that he had to shut off when it grated on his nerves, and he attempted to read, but his mind couldn't stay focused.

He held it together when Mike came to visit after work. Rafe managed to talk about his mother's visit and her new glasses. His brother seemed to sense his edginess because he didn't push or ask about Sheena. He didn't even invite Rafe to supper, which was fine.

As soon as Mike headed back across the yard, Rafe broke. He released the pent-up emotions he'd held too long. He wept and sobbed. His grief for the life he might have had fueled those tears, and all the frustrations of civilian life were vented. He cried for a long time, sometimes pounding the pillows on his bed and shouting into them.

But when the outburst ended, he had something he hadn't had for a long time. It was something fragile and small but there.

It was hope.

He wanted to cling to it and keep it.

Rafe just had a hard time accepting it could be his.

Chapter Four

For the rest of the week, Rafe holed up in his apartment like a hibernating animal. He talked to Mike the few times his brother invaded his space. In the late hours when he had trouble sleeping, he sometimes drove to the twenty-four-hour discount store to restock his essentials. He bought a hooded sweat jacket and wore it, so people couldn't view his face as easily. Although he had worked there recently, he avoided his former coworkers.

On the day before Halloween, he bought several bags of candy and made up treat bags for Matthew and Catherine, then three more for Eamon, Deirdre, and Sean. Twice, he headed over to the house when only his mom would be home.

She poured him coffee and offered cookies.

When she reported she'd had no more headaches, he rejoiced. But when she asked if he would come to church on Sunday, Rafe told her no and stayed home. He checked a few job sites online with little real interest.

He sent the candy over to the kids through Mike and stayed inside, reading. Halloween was one night he wouldn't venture out. November arrived with cooler temperatures, heavy rains, and some wind. Most of the radio stations switched over to holiday music, and when Rafe tried to watch television, every other commercial had a Christmas tree or Santa or something. When he went to the grocery store, the red and green of Christmas trumped Halloween's orange and black.

Rafe often thought about Sheena. He replayed their short time together in his mind. The moment when she touched his cheek haunted him. Her touch and kindness seemed so real, and he wanted it to be genuine. Sometimes he believed it, and sometimes he doubted. What if he misread her? Maybe she hadn't been as blind to his injuries as he thought. Sheena's emotion might have been pity. He considered a trip to the bookstore but chickened out. And he thought about going to church, but again, he changed his mind. He wanted to know what Sheena thought about him, but at the same time, Rafe didn't.

At the end of the first week of November, Mike arrived with a big box tucked under one arm and barged into the apartment. "Hello, Rafe. How's it going?"

Rafe sighed, resenting the intrusion. "Same as always. I get through one day at a time."

"I thought maybe you'd come back to church. You seemed like you enjoyed it. And they're putting together a Christmas choir. You used to sing at church." Although Mike spoke the truth, it wasn't something Rafe wanted to hear.

Rafe shrugged. "I don't know. I doubt anyone wants to look at Quasimodo singing carols."

Mike frowned. "I see you're back at it."

"At what?"

"Oh, never mind. Did you find a new job yet?" His brother, still toting the box, sat on the couch without waiting for an invitation.

"You know I haven't, Mike." Rafe resisted the

urge to roll his eyes and ask Mike to leave him alone. His brother wore the same exasperating expression he'd had as kids when he wanted to spring something big onto Rafe, usually something he would rather not do.

"Don't you want to know what's in the box?"

Here it comes. "No, I don't."

"Well, you will when you see what it is." Rafe watched as Mike opened the box and pulled out a full Santa Claus suit. "Ta-da!"

Rafe cringed. "What is it?"

Mike grinned and held out the suit. "It's a top-of-the-line Santa Claus outfit. This is the best. Look at the velvet jacket and pants, the faux ermine fur trimmings, the leather belt, and the matching boots. Jolly Old St. Nick himself couldn't dress any better than this."

Rafe quit believing in Santa at the age of seven. He would rather be in uniform than wear the ridiculous getup. "Then take it to the North Pole."

Mike ignored his request and beamed. "It's for you. I got you the best job ever. You're gonna love it."

Realization brought horror. Rafe's stomach tied into a knot. "Oh, no, you don't. I'm not playing Santa Claus, Mike. It's not happening."

His brother's smile wilted. "Come on, you love Christmas."

Rafe balled his fists. "No, correction: I *used* to love Christmas when I had a face and a life. It's just another day on the calendar to me."

"You'll be fantastic."

Rafe resisted the urge to punch the wall. "Mike, what are you talking about? What is all this about?"

"I told you I'd find you a job, right?"

He hadn't thought Mike really would. "Yeah, you

did."

"This is it!" Mike sounded excited, but his enthusiasm wasn't catching.

Rafe blew air through his nose and asked the obvious. "Do you want me to play Santa?"

His brother offered a grin and shouted, "Yes!"

Nothing sounded less likely than donning the suit and playing the old elf, but he asked, for Mike's sake, "Where would this be? Is it at your office Christmas party or at church or what?"

"Oh, it's even better. It's at the mall!!" Mike put the suit back into the box.

Rafe's recent experience at the mall had triggered an episode. It had also given him a chance to interact with Sheena, but he doubted he had the courage to brave it again, especially not as Santa Claus. "You're outta your mind. I hate the mall."

"No, you don't. Mom said you hung out, went to the food court and all when she got her glasses."

Rafe came to his feet. It was time to admit the truth. "Mike, I freaked out."

Mike stood. "She said you were sitting with Sheena Dunmore."

"So?" He lifted his eyebrows, trying to be casual and convince Mike spending time with Sheena didn't matter.

"So, you survived the mall," Mike stated. "It's a great job, Rafe. The pay is excellent for the season. And it's short term, November through Christmas."

Rafe could use some cash inflow, but he still found the idea ridiculous. "How good is excellent?"

"It's eight hundred a week to start. If you do a fantastic job, they'll up your pay even more."

He must have heard wrong. Rafe paced the length of the room twice, then faced his brother. "You're crazy. I look more like some evil Santa thing—what is it, Krampus—than I do Kris Kringle. I'm not old or fat, but I have scars."

Mike reached deeper into the box. "It comes with body padding, Rafe. And this is the deluxe wig and beard. It's so soft—wanna touch it? It will cover your bum ear and the worst of your scars. If you're wearing the whole outfit, kids aren't going to notice a few scars, and besides, Santa is *old,* so it won't be a big deal to them."

Rafe still resisted the idea, but it had some appeal. First, he'd be at the same mall where Sheena managed the bookstore. He'd have the chance to see her, every day. The Santa getup provided a disguise. She wouldn't know it was him unless he told her, and Mike had a point. His disfigurement wouldn't be so obvious wearing the costume. He had to admit, the money would be welcome. He had few needs and received minimal disability payments from his Marine service but earning some additional money appealed. "How do I know I could even get this job if I apply?"

"You don't have to apply—it's yours if you want it." Mike headed for the door, still grinning.

Something didn't fit, and Rafe needed to know what. "How so?"

"Okay, here's the total truth. The mall has hired the same guy to play Santa for the last five or six years. He had a triple bypass last week, so he's not available. Santa arrives at the mall on Saturday for the season, and they need someone to replace him. I'm in Exchange Club with the mall manager, Steve Kristoff. He's a

Marine, by the way, and he mentioned something about being in a bind without Santa. So, I told him about you. He said the job is yours if you want it. So, what do you say?"

Rafe thought about it. He consulted the calendar. "Saturday is *tomorrow,* Mike."

"I know." Mike's expression never changed.

Rafe had been blindsided. "Couldn't you have given me a little more notice? I'd want to think about it."

Mike, hand on the door, turned back to face Rafe. "I know I should have, but I was waiting for the suit to get here."

It sounded plausible for about three seconds. "Wait—didn't the mall already have a Santa costume?"

His brother didn't meet Rafe's gaze. "It belongs to the guy, and I promised if they offered it to you, I'd buy a new suit."

Rafe didn't know if he wanted to punch his brother or hug him. "You spent money for this thing?"

"Yes."

"And you didn't know if I would say yes or no?"

Mike shrugged. "I was hoping you'd do it."

"And if I don't, you're out the price of this thing." Talk about emotional blackmail.

Mike sighed. "I can try to sell it on eBay or something. Are you mad? I'm just trying to help you, bro."

Rafe sat, feeling cornered, and if hadn't been for the fact he'd see Sheena, he would have refused. The weekly pay sweetened the pot. "I'm not angry. And I know you're all about helping me but give me more notice next time, would you?"

The first hint of a smile returned to Mike's lips. "Are you going to do it?"

Rafe drew in a long, deep breath and then exhaled it fast. "Yeah, I'll do it. I'll try it. If it doesn't work out, then I'm gonna quit. Since you went to a lot of trouble, I'll do it. I might hate it, and if I do, you'll hear about it."

"I can live with your decision."

If Mike's grin got any wider, Rafe might be tempted to wipe it off his face. He was a Marine and knew how to throw a punch. Resigned, he scrubbed his face with both hands and accepted the reality. "Tell me where I have to be tomorrow and all the details."

At a quarter till ten on Saturday morning, Rafe perched on top of a fire truck, lights flashing and sirens blaring, as they approached the main mall entrance. Dressed in the Santa garb from hat to boots, he doubted anyone would recognize him. As the truck rolled to a stop, a large crowd cheered, and for once, although the attention focused on him, Rafe could be confident it wasn't because of his scars or disfigurement.

Nervous bats—because they were too big to be butterflies—flapped around in his gut, but a sweet sense of anticipation almost overrode it. In high school, way back before he joined the military, he had been in a couple of stage productions. Teenage Rafe had gloried in all the theatrical fun. He'd loved the applause and the cheers. He had almost forgotten, but now, as kids waved and people of all ages cheered, he remembered that he had liked playing a role.

Rafe Sullivan shied away from crowds and hated mirrors. But put him into a red velvet suit, add a mane of white hair and a flowing beard long enough to make

ZZ Top proud, and his inhibitions vanished. Rafe might dislike such things, but Santa Claus basked in all of it. Climbing down from the fire truck and strutting into the mall while a high school choir sang "Santa Claus Is Coming Town" gave him a chance not to be a Marine or disfigured or suffering from PTSD. He became the mythical, magical elf who delivered Christmas presents around the world each December twenty-fourth. And in those moments, he almost forgot Christmas hadn't been a thing for him in a long time.

When he first saw the line snaking down the length of the main mall alley and doubling back, he cringed. But once he mounted the raised platform and settled into the oversize throne fit for royalty, Rafe settled down. At this point, he didn't dare have a meltdown.

It helped when he spotted Sheena hovering in the doorway of the bookstore, watching, and waved one mitten. She shot him a smile, as if she knew who hid behind the Santa persona. She couldn't, though. Mike had promised no one except Gabe and Mom and the mall manager would know about this gig.

"Are you ready, Santa?" Tiffany, one of two college students who served as Santa's elves, asked.

Rafe took a long, slow breath. "Ready as I'll ever be, so let's get this thing started."

The first kid to sit on his lap giggled and preened. For a moment he panicked, certain he could not do this. He glanced around the mall, searching for an exit, and saw Sheena still there. Rafe focused on her to ground his fears. *Remember, right now everyone who sees you thinks of you as Santa. They don't see the battle-scarred veteran or Rafe Sullivan. No one knows who I am under the suit, and they don't care.*

He had to force the first "Ho, ho, ho," up from his belly, but when the little girl laughed, he relaxed. Rafe spent the next four hours listening to kids tell him what they wanted to find under the Christmas tree. Some were quite modest—a toy road grader or race car set, a baby doll, or pretend dishes—but some asked for an entire catalog of playthings. A few found Santa scary, but most calmed down once he talked to them a little and bounced them on his knee. More of them than he expected tugged on the beard to see if it was real, but since Mike paid for the deluxe version, it held.

From ten a.m. until two p.m., Rafe played Santa. He put on a smile for pictures, promised kids they would get what they wanted for Christmas, reminded them to behave, and laughed with them. At first, it had to be forced, but once he settled down, Rafe laughed for real. The last child before his sole break reminded him of child movie star Shirley Temple. Ringlet curls framed her face, and she demonstrated amazing energy, even star quality as she hammed up the experience for her parents. At the end, though, after Rafe promised—after a discreet thumbs-up from Dad—to deliver a doll house, tap shoes, ballet shoes, and a pink tutu, the little girl leaned up and kissed him on the cheek before climbing down from his lap. In her bright young voice, she blew him away.

"I love you, Santa. Thank you, and Merry Christmas!"

Her kiss landed between his faux beard and his right eye, in the center of his facial scars. It came close to the spot Sheena had touched, and the child's affection moved Rafe almost to tears. She couldn't be more than six or seven, close to his nephew Matthew's age, the kid who promised he would "have his six."

Tiffany the Elf changed the sign to read *Santa Will Be Back In Thirty Minutes* "Break time. I think we've earned it, too."

Relief spread through him. He was more than ready. "Aw, it wasn't so bad. But I'm glad to take a few minutes."

The down time presented a dilemma he hadn't considered. If he headed for the food court dressed as Santa, he would be mobbed in seconds. The same would happen if he headed to the restroom. *I guess I'll spend time in the mall employee break room.*

Rafe had no plans to remove his getup and reveal his identity. He hadn't packed lunch, either. He stepped down from Santa's big chair. If he remembered, the break room was located near the mall offices. He hadn't gone far when Sheena fell into step beside him.

"How's it going so far, Santa?"

He decided to stay in character. "Ho, ho, ho, it's been wonderful today."

Her eyes narrowed, but her smile never wavered. "I'm glad. Are you headed to the food court?"

Since that was the last place he wanted to go, he shook his head. "No, I'm on my way to the break room. Santa, uh, left his lunch money in the sleigh."

"What a shame. Well, Santa, if you want to step into the bookstore, I'd be happy if you'll eat in my office. I have extra food, just in case you wanted to join me. And there's even a small restroom so you can wash up if you want."

Did she suspect, or was she just being kind? Rafe wasn't sure. "Well, I appreciate the offer, young lady, but I'm not sure. I might need to feed the reindeer too."

A giggle escaped her mouth. "I'd be happy to give them their corn afterward, Rafe, if you want to join me. So, what do you think?"

A burst of happiness rushed through him. "How'd you know it was me? Did Mike tell?"

Sheena shook her head. "I recognized your eyes."

Skeptical, he tried to gauge her expression. "I don't believe you did, not with me done up like Old St. Nicholas. How could you?"

She giggled again and linked her arm through his. "I don't know but when I saw your grand entrance, I thought to myself that Santa was about the same height as Rafe Sullivan. I know the former Santa is out this year. You— I mean, Santa— did seem a lot rounder, but something about the way you moved kept me curious. When you first reached the throne, you were anxious, which made me suspect even more. When I got a good look at your eyes, I knew it was you under all the red velvet and fur."

Her perception surprised him, and he liked the way she'd taken his arm. Few people touched him casually these days. "Maybe Santa also has blue eyes."

"He might but not like yours. You have the prettiest eyes, Rafe, such a deep blue, almost indigo. They're so expressive."

He snorted. "And the right one is boogered up. If you recognized me at all, it's probably why."

She slacked her grip on his arm. "It's not. So do you want to eat with me or what?"

The way she asked wasn't rude or intense, just matter of fact. He'd imagined talking to Sheena again and now that he was, he'd been abrasive. A little ashamed since that wasn't what he wanted, he tried to fix it. "I do, Sheena, thanks."

Her smile returned. "Then come with me."

She led him through the bookstore, a typical chain outlet with a lot of new releases and titles from popular authors. Toward the rear of the store, a short hallway had public restrooms and an unmarked door. It opened into her office. The small, windowless space held a desk, an office chair, two chairs and a small table. Sheena sat at the desk and waved her hand.

"Grab a seat. I hope you like cheeseburgers and fries."

Rafe studied the food. He wondered how he would get the beard off so he could eat without smearing grease or mustard or cheese on it. "I do," he said.

She glanced up. "But? Is there a problem?"

There were several. "No but I haven't figured out how I'm going to eat without getting stuff all over the beard."

"Is it glued in place?"

"No, definitely not."

Sheena waved one hand. "Then take it off."

When he hesitated, she came around the desk to stand beside him. "Let me help. It's not hooked over your ears or anything, is it?"

"No, it's not." Surely, she had noticed he had one ear, not two.

Sheena ignored his remark. She removed the hat, then the wig, with gentle hands. "Oh, this is easy," she told him, as she lifted the elastic strap holding it in place. "There you go."

Rafe hadn't realized how hot he'd been until the hair and beard were gone. He ran a hand through his matted hair. "Thanks. Let me say a blessing and then we can eat."

His break went fast. The still-warm burger and fries filled his stomach, but he didn't dare drink all the cola. Santa didn't get many restroom breaks. "Everything tasted good. I appreciate it."

"No biggie. How long do you play Santa today?"

He answered her question without any fuss." Until seven tonight. Then I work tomorrow noon till six and then ten until seven the rest of the week."

Sheena lifted her eyebrows. "You have quite a schedule. Don't you get a day off?"

He should have asked but hadn't. "I don't know."

She waggled her fingers. "You should. They need to hire another Santa so you can."

Rafe shrugged. "Maybe but I doubt they will. The job's only for a few weeks, if I stick it out."

"Why wouldn't you?" She cocked her head.

A dozen excuses popped into his head, but he answered with the truth. "I have a bad track record of quitting jobs."

"Oh." She didn't ask why or sound like it shocked her. "Are you going to church tomorrow?"

Rafe hadn't planned to go, but maybe he would, now. "I hadn't thought about it."

"Well, if you do, I'll see you there. There's about five minutes left. Would you like me to help put your hat and hair back on?"

He resisted an urge to pull away. He hated to seem helpless. "I can do it."

Her hands were on his head before he could refuse. "So can I, Rafe. Let me."

Before he could protest, Sheena replaced it all. Her proximity made him nervous. Rafe inhaled the scent of her perfume. Her hair swept across his arm, ticklish and tempting. Her nimble fingers put everything back together. He hadn't been this close to any woman who wasn't a nurse or a relative since his injuries. And he liked it, maybe a little too much. "Thanks."

"You're welcome. I'll see you around, maybe at church and here at the mall. Take care, Rafe." Sheena lifted her hand to cup his cheek.

Touched, he hoped he wasn't blushing. "Thanks for the meal. Have a good rest of the day."

The rest of his shift went quickly with a steady stream of kids of all ages. They sat on his lap, whispered in his ear, shouted their requests to everyone, and posed for pictures. By the time the last child departed, Rafe's head pounded from the heat, the noise, the tension, and the camera flash. In the break room, he shed the suit, folded it into his assigned locker, and headed for his car. On the way home, he picked up a salad and some chicken tenders.

Mike ambushed him on the stairs to his apartment, grinning and eager. "How'd it go?"

His enthusiasm had waned. Now he was tired and his steps dragged. Rafe's head ached from the long day. "It went."

"So how was it?"

Rafe wanted to work up some enthusiasm, however fake, but couldn't, not in the face of his brother's relentless questions. "Intense. It was harder than I thought and longer. I sweat like a pig in the suit."

Mike raised his eyebrows. "Was it all bad? I thought maybe you'd like it."

Rafe shrugged. "I liked some of it, and it was all right."

"Good to know, brother. So, you won't quit tomorrow?"

The temptation loomed strong, but he thought about Sheena and shook his head. "No, I'll hang in there for now, Mike. I'm tired, though, and I've got a rotten headache. I'm gonna eat and go to bed."

Nothing could tarnish his brother's enthusiasm. "Okay, sounds like a plan. I'll see you tomorrow, kid."

Kid. His brothers had often called him "kid" during childhood—sometimes with love, sometimes as an insult. It had always reminded Rafe that he was the youngest and that he couldn't do all the things Mike and Gabe did no matter how much he'd wanted to join them. Now, though, he accepted it as an affectionate nickname. "Sure, Mike. Good night."

Although weary, he lay awake long into the night, thinking about the job and more about Sheena Dunmore. Rafe considered attending church. It would delight his mother and please his brothers. And he would see Sheena. In the early morning hours, just before he drifted asleep, he decided he would go, if he woke up in time.

Sunlight bathed the bedroom with light when he awoke, too late for church. He had just enough time to make toast, drink a cup of coffee, clean up, and head out for another Santa shift.

The difference between today and the day before was that now Rafe thought he had a shot at doing this thing. He might even enjoy it.

Chapter Five

At the end of his first full week playing Santa Claus, Rafe had embraced moments he loved and endured many he hated. But he hadn't quit, and that was a victory. Although he hated to admit it, he enjoyed the role more than he ever imagined. Most of the kids were adorable and so sweet in their innocence. They made up for the handful of spoiled brats who kicked him or pulled his beard too hard or were rude. Two small ones had wet on Rafe, and another had vomited, but most of the spew had hit the floor, not his suit.

The hours were long, and he had learned there would be no other Santa. No days off, the manager told him. Although he always experienced some pain in the leg with the intramedullary rod made of titanium, it had increased with his activity. Sitting for hours at a time made his joints stiff, and the knee pain common in anyone with a titanium rod became almost constant. For the first time since his return to civilian life, Rafe had determined to tough this one out and to be a Marine, even if he wasn't in the Corps anymore. He spent his evenings with a heat pad on his knee and dosed the discomfort with ibuprofen.

Rafe saw Sheena daily. Sometimes they exchanged greetings, and most days they shared a meal. So far, no one else outside a few family members and Sheena knew about his job. When he was with her, Rafe always expected he might catch her staring with revulsion. So far, however, she hadn't but by now, she must have noticed. Rafe wondered why she said nothing about it.

With the long-sleeved red tunic and the wig, beard, and hat, most of his scars weren't evident. A few of the kids, however, noticed the lines etched into his cheek. One little boy traced them with one finger. "Santa had a boo-boo!" A young lady of ten, old enough that Rafe suspected she probably didn't believe in Santa, touched his face. "What happened?"

Aware that the idea Santa had been a Marine wouldn't match the traditional Santa Claus lore, Rafe had said, "One of the reindeer accidentally kicked my cheek."

The girl frowned, and her eyes filled with doubt. "Okay, if you say so."

One adult mentioned his drooping eye, but she hadn't seemed to realize it represented permanent damage. "Santa looks awfully tired," she'd told her twins vying for space on his lap. "Tell him what you want, and we'll let him go home."

Since the matched pair was the last in line for the evening, her words made sense. As she left, Rafe said, "Thanks."

The woman, who might have been an older mother or a younger grandma, offered him a smile. "Oh, don't mention it. My eye gets lazy when I'm super tired, too. I hope you get some rest."

Rest wouldn't repair his permanent damage but as Santa, he forced a smile. "I will." Rafe found that he could function in the spotlight and even enjoy it at times. Despite his aching knee and fatigue, he had more energy, and his mood became lighter most of the time.

He caved and told his family they could count on him to join them at Thanksgiving. Twice he caught himself whistling and several times, he sang along with music—always country, never Christmas—on the radio. He anticipated each interaction with Sheena and enjoyed her company more each day.

She possessed a fine wit and a cheerful way of making light of things that might bring someone else down. Sheena liked to laugh and often did. She ran the bookshop with kindness and skill, although she had confided sales were down. "A lot of the bigger bookstore chains have closed stores. I'm always worried something of the sort might happen here."

So did he, and Rafe wished he could find some positive words to offer. "I hope not."

Rafe had found her beautiful from the first day he spotted her at the harvest dinner, but he now understood she was just as lovely within. She dressed in pretty clothes but with a ladylike modesty he appreciated. Sheena garnered more attention in simple skirts and high-necked blouses than some women in tight jeans and tighter sweaters. Her faith wasn't just for show, either. He'd watched her in church, and the joy on her face during the service couldn't be faked. He liked her, a great deal. He needed a friend, and he lacked the courage to hope for anything more.

On the third Saturday in November, the hours dragged past. A cold rain had fallen throughout the day, heavy at times, and the weather forecast called for the possibility of sleet or snow overnight. His knee ached worse than usual, so much that he occasionally rubbed it despite the fact it didn't ease the pain at all. Although Thanksgiving wasn't until Thursday and the traditional

Black Friday kickoff of the shopping season was still almost a week away, the mall crowds had increased. More shoppers walked past carrying bags, and more parents brought their children to visit with Santa. Rafe had adjusted to the foot traffic, but as it grew, doubts began to surface again. If it hadn't been for the chance to see Sheena daily, quitting would have seemed like a viable option.

Although his elves, Tiffany and Becca, had put the velvet ropes in place to limit the lines by a quarter till two, enough kids were in place that Rafe didn't get his break until almost three. Since Sheena's break didn't always coincide with his, he had packed lunch all week. A ham and cheese sandwich, a bag of chips, and two of his mom's snickerdoodles were tucked into the mini-fridge in Sheena's office. He made his way over to the bookstore with a conscious effort not to limp.

Sheena was at the cash register, a pencil tucked behind her ear, her hair awry and tumbling down.

"Go on back. I'll join you if I can break away for a few minutes. We've been quite busy today."

"So has Santa. I'll understand if you don't make it." He would be disappointed if she couldn't.

Rafe visited the restroom and emerged with clean hands. After hours of handling kids, they were often both sticky and dirty. Then he managed to remove the hair and beard. Before he unpacked his lunch, he took several ibuprofen tablets, hoping they might relieve his pain. Since he didn't expect Sheena, he pulled the other chair over and propped his leg on it. He ate his sandwich, although he wasn't hungry and the cookies, waiting for the pain reliever to knock the discomfort down. Afterward, he put the blue ice pack from his lunch on his knee and rubbed the joint, willing it to stop hurting. Rafe shut his eyes and leaned back, grateful for the break. He might have dozed because he didn't hear Sheena come into her office until she spoke.

"Rafe, what's the matter?"

She sounded concerned, and he savored it, which was funny, because he'd gotten tired of his family fussing over him. *It's different with a woman, though.* "My knee's giving me a little trouble. It hurts some but I'm fine."

A frown took the place of her usual smile. "You don't appear to be doing all that great. Is there anything I can do?"

Sheena sounded so sincere he summoned up a smile. "No, but thanks."

She cocked her head as she considered it. "I probably could help somehow, but I doubt my staff could manage the store without me today. Is this a common problem with your knee?"

Rafe nodded. "Yeah, it is since the docs put in a titanium rod from the knee down. And there's not much I can do about it. The colder weather doesn't help. Once I get home this evening, I'll rest and doctor it."

"Why don't you come over after work? I'll fix supper for you, and you can take it easy," Sheena asked.

Her invitation startled him. The old Rafe would have accepted immediately, but he needed a moment to collect his thoughts. No one outside his family had asked him to join them for a meal since his return from the military. Rafe wondered if it was a friendly gesture or if this amazing woman might be interested in a relationship with a broken down specimen like himself.

He wanted to accept, but he hesitated. "I don't know. I like the idea, but I don't get out much."

He didn't know where she lived or with who or what her idea of supper might be. Rafe didn't want to make a mistake, either, assuming more than friendship might be offered. If he allowed it, he could fall hard for Sheena, and if she didn't feel the same, he'd be crushed. *I don't need a broken heart along with everything else.*

Sheena reached over and touched his hand. "You should come eat supper with us. I get off at four, so I'll have plenty of time to go home and cook. Do you like stuffed peppers? It's what I'm planning to make."

He almost drooled at the idea. He liked the dish and hadn't eaten any in forever. But he wondered who us might be. "I'll come, but don't go to any trouble for me. I'll be happy with anything."

She shook her head and shot him a smile. "Gran likes a nice Saturday night supper. She always made one for Pop, so I've continued the tradition."

Rafe backtracked. "If your grandmother is coming over, you don't need me."

The last thing he would want was to be on display. His appearance brought his own grandma to tears, and he didn't want to shock anyone.

Sheena put her hand on his shoulder. "Rafe, I live with my grandma. I thought you knew since she's friends with your mom. So, it's not a big deal. Gran and I are going to eat whether you come or not, but I wish you'd join us. Otherwise, I bet you'd just go home and heat something in the microwave."

She nailed it. "I was planning on canned hot tamales. But stuffed peppers sound pretty good, so okay. I'll come. What time? He couldn't believe he had committed himself. The moment the words left his mouth, he wanted to take them back. Funny thing was, Rafe really wanted to go. Even if Mrs. Gallagher stared, he craved time with Sheena, and he admitted he was nosy enough that he wanted to see where she lived.

"Awesome! I'm glad you said 'yes,' Rafe. We'll eat at seven thirty."

His break had to be almost over. "Give me your address. I need to get back to work." He took the piece of paper she scribbled it on and folded it. Then he put it in his billfold so he wouldn't lose it. His rattled nerves made him a little clumsy and distracted. Rafe worried about what he would say, what Sheena's grandma might think of him, and whether he had forgotten his social skills. He muddled through the remainder of his shift. He'd almost calmed down when Sheena walked by after four.

She waved. "Don't forget. I'll see you at seven thirty."

When his shift ended, he hurried to get out of the Santa suit. He decided the shirt he had worn to work was threadbare. Rafe bought a brand-new long-sleeved Henley at the department store and changed into it. On the way to the parking lot, he realized that if he didn't come home, Mike would probably worry. He might even come searching. Although he seldom used the cell phone his brothers had insisted he carry, Rafe called his brother.

Mike answered immediately. "Everything okay, Rafe?"

"Yeah, everything is fine, and I'm good. I, uh, just wanted to tell you I'm having dinner with a friend, so I won't be home until later."

There was a pause. Since he'd come home, Rafe hadn't had any friends over or gone out with anyone, something Mike knew so it was no surprise he questioned him.

"Bro, I know I'm going to sound overprotective and intrusive here, but what friend?"

Rafe drew a deep breath. "It's Sheena Dunmore, Mom's friend Mrs. Gallagher's granddaughter. She invited me over for supper."

Mike laughed. "Awesome! Go and have a good time."

"It's not a big deal." It was to Rafe, but he didn't want a lot of hoopla over it even though Mike sounded pleased.

"It is for me, brother. When you said you weren't coming home, I was worried you might be freaking out or something. So, I'm happy for you. What?"

His mother said something in the background.

"Here, tell Mom, would you? Then go on, don't be late."

Anne Sullivan's voice sounded hesitant, and he figured he'd managed to worry her—again. Sometimes he wished she would chill out a little—that they all would.

"Raphael? Son, what's going on?"

Rafe made plans to chew his brother out, big time, for putting their mother on the line. "I'm going over to eat supper with Sheena and Mrs. Gallagher. Sheena invited me, and I called so none of you would worry."

Next time, he wouldn't phone. He would just go and let them wonder where he was—if there was a next time. Probably wouldn't be once Grandma got a good look at his face.

"How wonderful, son. I'm glad you called." Rafe noticed her tone had lightened with the information. "Enjoy yourself."

Rafe hoped to. "I will, Mom. Bye."

Light sleet ticked against the windshield as Rafe read the address from her note. He knew the location and headed there. Ten minutes later, he parked in front of an old, narrow frame house. It seemed small compared to the home where he'd grown up—a rambling place built for a large brood. This dwelling had been built a long time ago, he guessed, for a workingman's family. On his way to the porch, he noticed how well-kept it appeared. A sudden burst of anxiety struck, and he almost bolted. Instead, he rang the doorbell so he couldn't.

Sheena answered, dressed in blue jeans and a sweatshirt. Her hair had been pulled back into a tight ponytail. "Hi," she said. "I'm glad you came. Come on in. Supper's not quite ready, but it won't be long."

Rafe followed her into a living room to the left of the front door. An elderly woman sat in a vintage recliner, and he recognized her from church. She looked comfortable, with her white hair pulled up into a bun.

Like Sheena, she wore jeans and greeted him with a smile. "Hello."

Sheena indicated Rafe, then her grandmother, waggling her hands in their direction. "Gran, this is Rafe Sullivan, Anne's youngest. Rafe, this is my grandmother, Gretchen Gallagher."

Rafe extended his hand. "I'm pleased to meet you, Mrs. Gallagher. I don't think we've met, but I've seen you at church." Gretchen shook hands with a surprising firm grip for an elderly lady.

"Likewise, young man. I've heard so many good things about you. You were in the Marines, weren't you, and saw combat?"

Just look at my face and you'll see the answer. "Yes, ma'am, I did."

"My husband would have enjoyed meeting you. He served in the army, in both World War II and in Korea. He joined when he was barely seventeen years old. He lied about his age to get in. If you look behind you, there's his picture."

Rafe studied the standard army pose, a sober-faced young man in uniform who stared straight ahead at the camera and nodded. "He must have been a fine soldier."

"Oh, he was," Gretchen said. "I waited and worried about him through two wars. He made it through his first war with nary a scratch, but he wasn't as lucky in Korea."

Curious about what she might mean, he didn't ask because Sheena spoke. "The timer just went off so if you need to wash your hands or anything, I'll get supper on the table."

"Where's the bathroom?" Rafe wanted to wash his hands.

"It's through the kitchen and one step off the enclosed back porch, unless you want to go upstairs."

By the time he returned, Sheena had food on the already set table. He recognized Blue Willow Ware dishes because his Aunt Nell had owned a set just like these. Rafe waited until Mrs. Gallagher sat at the head of the table and gestured for Sheena to have a seat. Once both women were in place, he joined them. His manners might be out of practice, but he remembered the basics.

Since he'd met Sheena at church, he expected her to say grace, but Rafe wasn't prepared when both women reached out and grasped his hands. The older woman's fingers held his hand tightly, her skin work-worn and smooth. Sheena's fingers wrapped around his and made him aware of her proximity.

"Rafe, would you ask the blessing?"

His mind went blank. He couldn't remember any of the words he had known since childhood, so he winged it, drawing the words from his past with slow concentration. "Thank you, Lord, for this food, and bless it as we share the meal together. Bless this house and the hands that prepared this dinner. Grant us your peace." He was certain he had babbled, probably sounded stupid.

But both women said, "Amen."

A few weeks ago, he had eaten chili dogs with his family, but Rafe couldn't remember the last time before that he had a home-cooked meal. The disastrous Thanksgiving might have been it, but he might not have enjoyed a delicious supper with his family since he had come home on leave before shipping out to the Gulf. It took an effort not to gobble, to use his fork, and to chew with his mouth shut.

The food proved to be delicious. Sheena's stuffed peppers were filled with a flavorful beef and rice mixture. The green pepper enhanced the taste of the meat. The mashed potatoes were homemade, lumps and all, with a thick brown gravy. Green beans simmered long enough to wrinkle with diced onions, and hot rolls completed the menu. Rafe had to pace himself so he wouldn't overeat and get a stomachache. He wasn't used to this much food at a meal.

Sheena made conversation as they ate. She kept on everyday topics, like the changing weather and the upcoming holidays. She and her grandmother discussed when to decorate their Christmas tree. Sheena voted for the weekend after Thanksgiving, maybe on Sunday after church, but Gram wanted to wait until December.

"I don't like rushing Christmas. I know things have changed, but I like to keep my Thanksgiving and Christmas separate. Things should be enjoyed in their own time, don't you think, Rafe?"

He swallowed a bite. "I hadn't thought much about it, Mrs. Gallagher. But I agree—let's keep turkey and the poinsettias separate."

Both women laughed. "When does your family decorate?"

The simple question took him by surprise. They did, he knew, but he had paid little attention to *when*. To answer, Rafe drew on his childhood memories. "They usually wait for the first Saturday in December."

Gram nodded her approval. "Sounds just right to me."

"Do you put up a small tree or anything for the holidays, Rafe?" Sheena asked in her calm, soft voice.

He shook his head. Then he put down his fork. "I haven't. There didn't seem to be much reason for just me."

"Oh, you should."

From the glint in Sheena's eyes, he figured she must be one of those people who adored everything Christmas and made a huge deal out of it.

"Celebrating Christ's birthday is the most joyous

time of year. I love it."

Rafe stared down at his plate. This didn't seem to be the moment to mention that since suffering his injuries and leaving the US Marine Corps, he didn't care for Christmas. He never listened to happy Christmas carols or watched sentimental holiday movies or the old classic Christmas kids' shows on television or did anything special. The last couple of years, he had trudged across the yard to exchange gifts with Mom and Mike's family without staying for dinner. He bought gift cards for everyone and handed them out on Christmas Eve or on Christmas. Playing Santa had made the holiday more tolerable, but it was one thing to put on a red suit and playact. It was another to celebrate and find a little Christmas in his heart. He might want to, he realized, but it wasn't there, and he didn't think it would be ever again. Somehow, he didn't think that was an opinion either woman would like. "It's nice." If Sheena noticed his lack of enthusiasm, she said nothing.

"Wait until the day after Thanksgiving. I know a few stores have put up some decorations, and of course there's the Santa Stop, but by Friday morning the mall will be transformed into a Christmas wonderland. It's gorgeous and so festive."

He forced a smile, trying to be more Santa than Scrooge, but Rafe didn't feel it. "I bet." Maybe she had caught on to his apathy.

Sheena didn't mention Christmas again, but she uncovered a huge chocolate layer cake. "I hope you saved room for dessert."

Without warning, Rafe couldn't breathe. The warm house, the wonderful food, the conversation, and talk of

Christmas combined to overwhelm him. Everything together proved to be too much for a social recluse, and he needed air. He considered escaping and rejected it. If he didn't like Sheena so much and if she hadn't been so kind, he would have bolted. But if he didn't get a few solitary moments, he would explode. "Sure. Chocolate cake is my favorite. I need to use the restroom first, though."

Without waiting for a response, Rafe shoved back his chair and scurried to the bathroom he had used before. It was rather small, but he shut the door and took huge, gulping breaths. He sat on the closed lid and rested his head on his hands. He struggled to process his emotions.

Sheena and her grandmother treated him as if he were normal. They didn't stare at his missing ear or his scars. Although he'd almost gotten used to hiding behind his Santa Claus suit, Rafe didn't know how to handle normalcy. Most of the time, his family walked on eggshells around him, probably always afraid they might offend him. Mike was the one occasional exception but even he babied Rafe too much.

In public, Rafe always had his guard up, ever vigilant for some chance remark or harsh word. He had spent too long expecting people to be rude and to judge him by his disfigurement. Rafe thanked God that there was no mirror in the tiny bathroom. Right now, he couldn't bear to gaze at his ugly face. It reminded him too much of what he had lost. He sat for five minutes, then ten, before he managed enough courage to splash water on his face. Before he returned, Rafe walked around the enclosed back porch. He noted that a washer and dryer covered an interior wall. Rafe noticed the cast iron black ranch style wood stove against the outside wall. Two worn rocking chairs and some shelves took the remainder of the space.

He steeled himself for his return. *Now they will gawk, and it's my fault. I did something out of the ordinary and reminded them I'm a freak.* Walking into the kitchen proved to be harder than he anticipated. He feared that the pleasant atmosphere would have vanished. He expected cold stares and hurt feelings but when he joined the two women at the table, there were neither.

A huge piece of chocolate cake rested on a small plate at his place. The leftovers were gone, probably packed into containers, and put into the fridge. The dirty dishes and pans were stacked near the sink.

"I cut your piece of cake."

Sheena's voice remained as sweet and friendly as before.

"We waited to have our dessert with you."

"Thanks." What else could he say? Rafe ate the cake, which happened to be the most fantastic, richest chocolate confection he had ever eaten. He managed to compliment Sheena and to navigate through more small talk. When he finished the cake, though, Rafe figured he had pushed his luck as far as it might go for one night. "Sheena, Mrs. Gallagher, thank you for inviting me. I enjoyed it and the food was wonderful."

The older woman beamed. "I'm glad you did, young man. Come back sometimes."

"I'd like to." Rafe realized he meant it. And he *had* enjoyed the food. It would have been a perfect evening if he hadn't gotten anxious. "I need to go, though. If it's still sleeting, the streets might be getting slick."

"I'll walk you out," Sheena told him.

He'd like that, a lot but he decided to be polite. "You don't have to."

Her gaze met his. "I want to."

Rafe shook Mrs. Gallagher's hand and mumbled good-bye. Then he headed toward the front door with Sheena at his heels.

She flipped on the light as they stepped onto the porch.

The earlier sleet had become big snowflakes. "It's cold. You should go back inside."

Sheena rubbed her arms and shivered. "I will, in a minute. Didn't you wear a coat?"

He'd come straight from the mall, and although he'd bought a shirt, he didn't see a need to buy a jacket, too. "No."

She stepped closer. "You should. You don't want to get sick. All those kids are counting on Santa being at the mall."

He laughed a little. "I'm fine."

Sheena put one hand on his arm. "Are you?"

Embarrassment flooded him. She had noticed when he freaked out, and he had so hoped she wouldn't. "I am, Sheena. I had a moment when everything kinda overwhelmed me, but not in a bad way. I'm not used to being with many people."

"I understand, Rafe. How's the knee?"

Her voice dropped low, softer than the falling snow. Rafe had almost forgotten about it with everything else. "Better, thanks for asking."

"Good. Will you be at church tomorrow?" The question came with a tentative smile.

Every week, she asked, and he considered it. But

he hadn't attended since the harvest dinner and probably wouldn't. "I don't know. I have to be at work at noon so it would cut the time pretty close."

"You could come to the early service at eight. I'll be there. Otherwise, I won't see you until Monday."

She sounds like she wants to see me. The possibility brought a strong sense of disbelief and a tiny hint of wonder if it was true. "Maybe I will. I can't promise, though, Sheena."

Her voice was soft. "Well, I hope I see you there."

Then to his surprise, she stepped forward and stood on tiptoe. Sheena leaned forward and cupped her hand against his right cheek, the damaged one. And she touched her mouth to his in the lightest kiss, a mere brush, but the first since he'd been evacuated out of the Helmand Province. His heart fluttered, and he had no idea what to say.

On instinct, he put his arms around Sheena and kissed her back, his mouth sweet and gentle against her lips. Then, before he managed to do or say something stupid, Rafe pulled free. He marched out to the car, climbed in, and chanced to look back.

Sheena stood framed in the open doorway, wearing a smile. She waved.

He lifted one hand to acknowledge it. He drove home on autopilot, his senses muddled and his mind preoccupied. Before he went to bed, though, he set his alarm because he decided he would attend early church in the morning.

And he would see Sheena.

Chapter Six

This time, Rafe wore his own clothes instead of Mike's. He chose his best jeans, his single button-down blue chambray shirt, and his boots. After coffee and toast, he headed for the church. Nervous did not begin to describe his emotions as he arrived well before the service and took up a seat in the back pew. A few people were present, but he didn't see Sheena. Rafe decided if she didn't show up, he would slip out as soon as the singing started. He couldn't sit still, waiting. His hands twisted together into knots. He bounced his left leg up and down. About the time the music began and the congregation came to their feet, he decided Sheena wasn't coming. As soon as the song began, he would split.

Before he did, she slipped into the pew beside him and lifted her voice with his in the first hymn. His spirits rose, and he sang with full strength and power, without reservation. Rafe clapped with the rhythm of the music, and by the time they sat to hear the sermon, he had relaxed. Sheena sat on his left side, something he enjoyed. She could see his profile and maybe she would imagine how handsome he had once been.

Midway through the service, she put her hand in his and held it.

Rafe savored the warmth of it and wrapped his fingers around hers. If things were different, if he were

68

the Rafe he used to be, he would dream of a relationship with this woman. Once, he had wanted a wife and family. He had surrendered those aspirations with his good looks and didn't dare hope anymore.

The sensation of their kiss last evening lingered, and he enjoyed their joined hands. They didn't talk much. There wasn't any opportunity during the service, and afterward, they talked to a few people. Most of them remembered Rafe from his youth, and although he hadn't been aware at the time, they had prayed for his recovery. The idea touched him on a deep level.

"I suppose you need to head for work." Sheena told him as they walked out into the parking lot. The snow hadn't accumulated, but little wisps blew across the pavement.

If he could, he would skip it, stay home, and read or beg for a Sunday dinner invitation. "Yeah, I do. It takes time to change into Santa Claus."

"Are you glad you came this morning?"

Rafe didn't hesitate. "Yes, I am. I enjoyed church and the company." The music and the lessons taken from Scripture uplifted him.

"Good. Well, I'm parked over there. I'll see you tomorrow at the mall, Rafe."

It seemed far distant. "Sure." He wondered if he might kiss her, if she'd mind, and decided maybe the church parking lot wasn't the right place. As if Sheena knew, she opened her arms, and he hugged her. Affection welled up within Rafe's heart, and he realized he might be falling in love. Bad idea, he thought, but he savored every moment spent with her.

Sheena walked to her vehicle.

He watched, smitten, unaware he wasn't alone until

Mike spoke. "You're full of surprises these days."

A warm feeling brought the realization he was happy. "Am I?"

"I had no idea you were up, let alone at church. Why didn't you come with the rest of us?" Mike wore a grin brighter than the sun.

Rafe shrugged. "I have to be at work at noon, so the late service doesn't work with my schedule."

Mike winked. "And maybe because Sheena Dunmore came to early church."

He could pretend her presence had nothing to do with it, but his brother would know anyway. Besides, he'd told the family he had dinner at her house last night. "It might be a factor."

All teasing vanished as Mike clapped a hand on Rafe's shoulder. "It's a valid reason, and I'm glad to see you getting out more. I need to go. I dropped Charlotte, Mom, and the kids at the door so I need to go find them before the service starts. See you later, bro. Have a good day."

Rafe's shift passed quickly. The mall proved to be almost as busy on Sunday afternoon as on Saturday, and he feared it would become increasingly hectic as Christmas approached. He listened to kids sharing their wishes for the holiday, and everything remained routine. Several children were bashful, but Rafe cajoled them into telling him what they wanted to find under the tree. At five till six, the last two kids approached his lap accompanied by their dad. Rafe noticed the military haircut and the ramrod posture. He pegged the guy for a fellow Marine, even before the man glanced at Rafe's hand.

"I should have known Santa was a jarhead. Did

you serve in Iraq or Afghanistan?"

"Both." He glanced down at his ring. It must be how the other marine recognized him. No way could anyone guess his appearance under the red suit and faux hair.

"I'm Samuel Wynkowski," the man said and stuck out his hand to shake. "So did I. Got out a couple years ago. I always planned to be a career Marine, but I changed my mind. I moved here eight months ago. What do you do now besides be Santa?"

Rafe hated questions, especially ones he couldn't answer. "I'm between jobs. This is a temporary gig. I'll be searching for a new one after the holidays. What about you?"

"I'm a law enforcement officer. I used the GI Bill to go through the Academy. The local police department has a lot of ex-servicemen. They could use another Marine, if you're interested."

He had tanked as a security guard, but law enforcement wasn't a field he had considered. His thinking had shifted, though. "I might be. I need to get into a career."

The other Marine nodded. "Keep it in mind. Oorah!"

The chance meeting and the idea lingered long after Wynkowski and his son had gone. His recent foray into the public and his interaction with Sheena convinced Rafe he needed to reclaim his life. At thirty-five, he couldn't remain a recluse forever. None of the jobs he had held had suited him or been a career. *Mike would like it, and Mom would be proud.*

He figured Sheena would be in favor, as well. When he had a chance, he might mention it and see what she thought. Rafe valued her opinion and believed she would give him an honest one.

On Monday, the family scattered. Charlotte left to drop Matthew and Catherine off at their elementary school and headed for the high school where she was subbing Modern World History all week. Mike had already gone to his insurance office, so Rafe wandered over to the house. He found Mom upstairs in her sewing room. It had been his bedroom growing up, but everything except the blue paint on the walls and the navy curtains had changed. His posters were long gone, and his remaining toys had been handed down to Matthew. He had come up here once, when he first came home, and never since.

His mother glanced up from sewing several scraps into a quilt block. "Hello, Rafe."

If she had any curiosity about why he'd come to the house or sought her out, it didn't show. "Hi, Mom. Is this a new quilt?"

Anne Sullivan nodded. "Yes, it's for Catherine. I'm making it for Christmas for her bed, in her favorite pinks and yellows. I don't know if I'll finish it in time, but I'm hoping so."

He still had a quilt she'd made him, folded at the foot of his bed. "It's pretty."

Her quick smile lit her features and removed years. "Thank you. I hope she thinks so."

The kid should consider herself lucky to receive a handmade gift. "I bet she will." Rafe took a seat in an old armchair he remembered had been in the living room during his childhood. "Mom, can I ask you something?"

She put down her sewing and nodded. "Of course,

son. You can ask me anything."

Her expression became solemn, and her worry line appeared, bisecting her forehead. *She expects it's going to be something bad, I guess.* He had planned to lead up to his question, but he changed his mind. "Do you think I'd made a good police officer?" Whatever she had expected, Rafe guessed that wasn't it.

Her mouth opened. "I think you would be good at anything you put your mind to doing, Raphael. Is law enforcement something you want to pursue?"

The more he considered, he thought so. "Maybe. I don't know yet."

Mom leaned forward, interested, and fully engaged. "What made you think of it?"

"I met a Marine at the mall yesterday. He's an officer with the police department now. And I don't know how to do much else. It might the closest thing I could find to being in the Marines."

Anne offered a small smile. "Do you think you could handle all the stress?"

Her simple question irritated him until he considered how he had acted for two years. Then he realized it was a practical one. "I'm handling working at the mall so far."

She smiled. "I know, and I'm proud of you, Rafe. Would you attend the police academy or what?"

"If I decide to do it, then yes, I would."

"Your brothers and I, the whole family, we'll support you in anything you want to do," she said. "If you do become an officer, you'll have to be comfortable with your appearance. I know right now the Santa Claus costume hides a lot, and it's given you more confidence to be out in public."

Her candid words surprised him. So did her insight. "It's something I'd have to think about."

"Have you mentioned it to Sheena yet?"

Rafe shook his head. "No. I thought I might, though."

"You should. She's an intelligent young woman. I'm glad you're seeing her, Rafe."

Seeing her sounded like a relationship, and he wasn't sure he was there, yet. Or would ever be. "We're friends, Mom."

His mother's smile widened. "I'm glad. Everyone needs friends, Rafe."

They talked of other things for a few minutes until he had to leave for work. "I need to go, Mom."

"I'm glad you came over and talked. I've missed you, Raphael. Mike tells me you are coming to Thanksgiving dinner. Are you?"

He had promised, and he wouldn't go back on his word. "Yes, I'll be here."

Her eyes sparkled.

He could tell his decision pleased her.

"Good. We'll eat at two."

"Two works for me. Are you making your homemade noodles, too?"

"I am if you want them, Rafe."

Her noodles were an old favorite. "I do." He hugged her before he left, encouraged by their conversation. The career idea intrigued and terrified Rafe. After two years spent in isolation, after a string of short-lived, dead-end jobs, the recent changes in his life were major. A new career would be huge and force him to face challenges, including his appearance. Change came hard for Rafe at the best of times, so he struggled to deal.

At the mall, he donned his Santa gear and stopped by the bookstore. Sheena greeted him with a warm smile, and they talked for a few minutes. His plans to bring up the possibility of becoming a law enforcement officer would have to wait until his break.

"My district manager is here today. I have to take her to lunch, and we'll be going over the stock, sales, and books all day. She leaves at six. If you want to get together at seven when you finish for the day, I'd like it."

"Sure." He could wait. "I guess it means no lunch break in your office."

Sheena's face fell. "I'm sorry but it does. Natalie, the district manager, tends to be picky about rules."

"No problem." He tried not to show his disappointment. On the Monday before Thanksgiving, the mall wasn't busy, and since older kids were in school, Rafe had a steady stream of babies and toddlers. The little ones were usually easier to handle than the older children, but today, they were a challenge. Several cried when their doting parents sat them on his lap, and one could not be comforted or cajoled.

The tot's mama retrieved her. "I'm sorry. I thought Kelsey would settle down once she saw you. She loves Santa," the woman apologized with a faint smile and a harried look.

I'm not Santa, and at her age, I doubt she has any idea who Santa is supposed to be.

His thoughts distracted him from the job, and he wondered about his growing affection for Sheena and where it could go, if anywhere. Rafe kept thinking about the Marine, Samuel, who suggested he consider a career as a cop. At five after seven, when Tiffany put out the *Closed* sign, Rafe lost no time in bailing from Santa's oversized throne.

Sheena met him in front of the bookstore. "I'm almost finished. Rick can close. I'll meet you in ten minutes, if it's okay."

"It's good." Right now, Rafe needed to shed the suit and chill a little bit. He emerged from the mall offices and the break room.

Sheena was waiting and slipped her arm through his. "I'm hungry. Do you want to get something to eat?"

That was exactly what he wanted and needed. "Sure."

"Is the food court okay or would you prefer somewhere else?"

He released a sigh. "Sheena, right now I'd rather not go to the food court. Do you know somewhere else with private booths?"

"I'm sure I do. Has it been a hard day?"

Her sympathetic voice soothed some of the tension that had his stomach knotted tight. "It's been a long one," Rafe said. "There were too many fussy kids, and I have a lot on my mind. What I could use is a day off."

"You'll have Thursday off for Thanksgiving. Can't you take another day off if you need it?"

"No, this is a full-time gig until Christmas Eve, and then it's over. I need to stick it out to the end."

She touched his cheek, the scarred one. "If I can do anything to make it easier…"

Rafe put his hand over hers, delighted with the caress. "You do. I've needed a friend for a long time."

Sheena gripped his arm. "You've got one and

more, Rafe. I think I know the perfect place. Do you want me to follow you there or what?"

He'd rather not miss a single moment with her. "Ride with me."

She nodded. "And you'll bring me back here after? Okay."

The place she directed him to proved ideal. Housed in a faux log cabin building, Joe Earl's offered burgers and barbecue. Tall wooden booths around the edges of the large dining area offered privacy. Rafe chose a corner booth, and once they were seated, only their server had a view. The lighting was dim but not dark, and he liked the ambiance. He positioned himself so his undamaged left side faced outward.

The old Rafe would have loved this place, old enough to have character with food delicious enough to please. The man he'd become since parting with the USMC liked it.

They ordered barbecued sandwiches - pulled pork for Rafe, smoked turkey for Sheena. When the meal arrived, the sandwiches were flanked with a generous portion of fries and a long dill spear. He picked up the meat-laden bun then hesitated as Sheena asked a quiet blessing. Rafe took the first bite and discovered edible heaven. "It's very good."

Sheena offered him a smile. "I knew you'd like it. Do you want to talk about your day?"

That was the last thing he wanted to discuss. "Not much."

She steepled her chin on one hand. "Then do you want to share what's on your mind?"

Rafe did and he didn't. Maybe she would think law enforcement would be a bad choice but unless he mentioned it, he would never know. "I'm thinking about what I'll do for a job after Christmas. I met another former Marine who became a police officer. He had the idea it might work for me as a career, too. I don't know what it takes to get into the academy, but I'm considering it."

Sheena nibbled a fry and wiped her hand on a napkin, nodding. "It sounds like it has some potential. Is it something you want to do?"

"I'm not totally sure yet but possibly."

Sheena leaned forward. "What did you do before you became Santa?"

He would bristle if anyone else asked the question, but Rafe answered Sheena with honesty. "Since leaving the Marines, I've bounced around in a lot of jobs. I quit as an overnight stocker at a discount store in October. I've mopped floors, loaded trucks, worked for a florist, was a security guard, dishwasher, and some other things." If he'd shocked her, it didn't show. Her expression didn't change.

"Did you enjoy any of the jobs?"

"No, I can't say I did. The only thing I know how to do is be a Marine, and there's not much call for those skills in civilian life."

She reached across the table to take his hand.

His heart did a flip.

"True. I suppose law enforcement would come closer than most."

That matched his thoughts. "It's along the lines of what I'm considering. What do you think?"

Her fingers wrapped around his hand. "If it's what you want and if it's right for you, then why not?"

Even though it was what he'd hoped to hear, the

barbecue he'd eaten so far soured in his belly. He couldn't skirt around his scarring any longer. "I can think of some obvious reasons."

Her expression never changed. "Like what?"

Rafe had a choice. He could step away from the painful issue of his damage and pretend it wasn't a factor. Hiding like an ostrich, though, was losing any appeal. As he searched for an answer, he recalled what one of his therapists at Walter Reed in Washington, DC had said. *As soon as you can talk about what happened, accept that you don't have a right ear, and the scars are permanent in an everyday way because you've accepted the reality, then the disfigurement loses its power. If you don't learn to talk about it, to accept it, then it will fester inside and cause more trouble.*

At the time, he had remained silent, and although Dr. Alexander Mooney had eventually shifted his attention toward someone who wanted help, he had listened. Now Rafe steeled himself to mention the obvious. "I have scars, terrible ones. I no longer have a right ear. Some of them are visible on my face, neck, down my arm, and on my body. You know about the trouble I have with my knee and leg. And you're aware I have PTSD. I don't know if any department would take on someone so damaged."

He didn't intend to spit out the words with such speed, but he did. Although his tone remained low, it became harsh. Rafe waited, expecting her to cry or leave or both. He hadn't meant to wound her, but he probably had. But Sheena surprised him.

She wiped her hands on a napkin and reached for his. "Rafe, honey, I'm not blind or stupid. Your scars and your ear aren't invisible, and I'd be lying if I said I never noticed. But they're also not as grotesque as you seem to think they are. Some people are mean. They stare and say things they shouldn't. And yes, you suffer from PTSD, and you have knee trouble. But none of it means you would be necessarily unfit to serve as a police officer. First, you have to decide if you want to go for it as a career. If it's right and you're accepted into the academy, and make it through, then it's the right thing for you. And there's one other thing you might do while you're wondering if you should or shouldn't try."

She had his full attention. "What's that?"

"Pray about it, Rafe. Leave it with the Lord and see what happens."

In a few sentences, Sheena acknowledged all his flaws and given him no pity. Maybe she failed to understand how difficult it had been to catalog his issues aloud. Rafe wanted to curl up into a ball. His chest hurt with the effort not to weep. In his hurt and to his dismay, he trembled. If he didn't get grounded fast, he would melt down in the middle of a restaurant with a woman who mattered to him. Rafe took a series of deep breaths and tried to focus. He replayed what she'd said. She had called him "honey." And when she talked about his injuries, she had been matter-of-fact about them. If he wasn't totally wrong, she cared.

Rafe struggled for control. He prayed, not about whether or not he should become a cop, but for calm. Rafe focused on how amazing that Sheena had never gazed at him with pity or scorn or ridicule. After a few minutes, he picked up his iced tea and drank some. The combined sugar and caffeine would help. And when he found the courage to glance across the table at her, she met his gaze "Thank you. It's what I needed to hear." Her words didn't hurt. Instead, he thought they might have begun an inner healing—something he'd long needed.

She sipped some tea and smiled. "I imagine so. Now if I haven't ruined our meal, let's finish eating."

He managed a shaky laugh as his appetite returned. "Sure."

Much later, after he had returned to his apartment, Rafe reflected on everything said. His physical wounds had healed long ago, but he still had a long distance to go with healing and dealing with the emotional baggage. And maybe, just maybe, he had taken a few tottering baby steps toward it tonight.

Chapter Seven

Two days remained until Thanksgiving and a brief respite from playing Santa Claus. Rafe dreaded the big holiday dinner with his brothers, their wives and children, his mom, Grandma Ruth, and probably as many other relatives as his mother could persuade to join them. At the same time, he anticipated the meal. Mom promised to have all the traditional dishes and some of his favorites. Young Matthew and Catherine were both excited about the holiday. Rafe had promised to come over to the house early so he could watch the Macy's Thanksgiving Day parade with the kids.

The number of shoppers and kids who wanted to see Santa dropped on Tuesday, and on Wednesday, the foot traffic was the lightest Rafe had seen. When he met Sheena for a late lunch, he mentioned it.

She laughed. "Everyone is probably at the supermarket instead of the mall, buying stuff for Thanksgiving."

"I hadn't thought about it but you're right." Since their meal at Joe Earl's, Rafe had relaxed his guard more than ever with Sheena.

"I'm looking forward to Thanksgiving but not to Black Friday," she told him as they ate chicken sandwiches. "I don't suppose you've ever been shopping on Black Friday."

He faked a shudder. Black Friday never had

appealed to him. Even before he'd been scarred, nothing sounded worse than fighting crowds to find discounts. "Never, not when I was in the corps and not since."

"It's going to be an experience, then. It gets intense. The whole weekend will be crazy."

He nodded. Right now, he would rather not think about it. "Are you going out of town for the holiday?"

Sheena's face changed. Her eyes narrowed, and she pursed her lips. "No." When she spoke, she raised her voice more than a little.

He wondered why. "Mom said you had moved here a few years ago. Where are you from?"

"I grew up in Tulsa," Sheena replied. "My parents still live there, but I'll be here with Gram."

"Are you making dinner?" Rafe thought he would rather partake of a small meal than face his extended relatives, if there might be an option. If he didn't go to Mom's, she would be disappointed but if Sheena invited him, he would consider accepting.

She frowned. "No. Didn't your mom mention it?"

"Mention what?"

"Anne invited Gram and me to join your family for Thanksgiving dinner. I thought she would have told you."

The unexpected news surprised him. Rafe would remember that. "No, she hasn't."

A faint worry line appeared on Sheena's forehead. "I hope you don't mind."

Rafe shot her a grin, and for once, he forgot to worry if the right side of his mouth drooping made it lopsided. Her presence would make what could be a difficult day emotionally a little easier. "I'm glad you'll be there, Sheena."

Relief brought a grin. "Good. I would hate to have to go home and tell Gram we had to eat frozen turkey dinners from the supermarket."

Since the mall closed early at six on the evening before Thanksgiving, Rafe had an extra hour free. He walked Sheena out to her car and lingered.

"Are you headed straight home?"

Her question caught him unaware. That was his plan. He needed some alone time to psyche himself for the holiday. "Yeah, I am. I'm tired."

Sheena touched his cheek with folded fingers. "You look it. Get some rest, and I'll see you tomorrow, Rafe."

"I'm looking forward to it. If you get there in time, you can watch the Thanksgiving Day parade on TV with me and the kids."

"That would be fun. I'll see—I have some baking to do first, either tonight or in the morning."

Baking interested him. He was fond of desserts, and that chocolate cake she'd made had been scrumptious. "What are you making?"

She shook her head and put a finger over her lips. "It's a surprise. Good night, Rafe."

He could wait to find out. "Bye, Sheena." Then, because he wanted to so much, Rafe put his hands gently on her shoulders. He bent down and kissed her, slow and sweet.

Sheena clasped her arms behind his neck and yielded to the moment.

The kiss lasted longer than his other effort, and Rafe wondered if she knew he hadn't kissed anyone else since before his injuries. When he stepped away, lips tingling with after-effects, there didn't seem to be anything else to say so he didn't try.

A few hours later, Rafe couldn't keep his mind on the story and he fell asleep over a book. He kept thinking about Sheena and how much he cared about her. They were friends, but he had a suspicion they were moving toward something deeper. He realized he had been falling in love with her since the first time he saw her, and if he were totally honest, he had already fallen. Love hadn't been something he expected to happen, and he needed to go slow so neither of them would get hurt.

He woke early on Thanksgiving and headed over to the house. Heavy clouds above threatened rain or snow soon. Rafe slipped in the back door and found his mom already at work in the kitchen.

"Good morning, son. There's coffee in the pot, chocolate milk in the fridge, and donuts on the dining room table, if you want some. The kids are already parked in front of the television, waiting for you."

"Thanks, Mom." He paused to kiss her cheek. Her eyes widened, and it occurred to him he hadn't been affectionate to anyone in a long time. Sheena had caused a change. Thinking of her prompted him to ask, "Why didn't you tell me Sheena and her grandmother are coming for dinner?"

Anne paused. "I thought I did."

Rafe might have believed her, but she refused to meet his gaze. "I would have remembered."

Mom gave a small laugh. "All right, so I didn't mention it. I was afraid you wouldn't come if you knew I invited more people. Are you unhappy?"

Rafe might not admit it, but he was thrilled. "No,

I'm glad, Mom. I like the idea of Sheena being here. Did you invite anyone else I don't know about?"

"I don't think so. The rest are all family."

"Okay." He poured a mug of coffee. "I'll be in with the kids, but if you need me to help with anything, give me a holler."

Mom kissed his unscarred cheek. "Thanks. Keeping Matthew and Catherine occupied is a huge help."

He picked up a couple of donuts—one chocolate frosted, one rolled in sugar and spice—on his way through the dining room. "So, have I missed anything yet?"

"Uncle Rafe's here!" Matthew shouted and dashed across the carpet to greet him. He still wore his footed action hero pajamas.

"Hi, Uncle Rafe." Catherine sat cross-legged on a pink beanbag chair. "It just started so no, you haven't."

Matthew tugged at his hand. "Sit with me down on the floor."

Rafe chuckled, pleased with the invitation. "Kid, if I get down so low I might never get up. My leg gets pretty stiff. Why don't you sit next to me on the couch for now?"

The kid nodded and changed position. "Okay."

Matthew snuggled up beside him as the parade coverage began. Rafe sipped his coffee and downed the donuts. He didn't have much interest in the parade although he enjoyed the marching bands. The kids' enthusiasm proved infectious, though, and he soon got caught up in their excitement, exclaiming over Mother Goose on one float and cheering for their favorite balloons as they appeared. When Santa made his end-of-the-parade appearance, Rafe said little, although Matthew, still young enough to believe in the old elf, prattled about how much he wanted to visit with Santa before Christmas.

"Mom says she'll take us to see him at the mall." Matthew dropped the bombshell.

Matthew's statement dropped on his uncle like a bombshell "Oh, did she?" Rafe hoped she wouldn't. If either of these two bright kids figured out his identity, it would be a disappointment.

Catherine nodded. "Maybe on Friday."

Mike came downstairs and joined them. "We'll see about it, kiddoes. Mom may have other ideas."

Matthew shook his head. "It was Mom who said we could."

Rafe found his voice. "Then you probably will."

During a commercial break, both kids made a chocolate milk run to the kitchen.

"Are you okay with the kids seeing Santa?" Mike asked.

Rafe shrugged. "I don't know. If it happens, I'll deal with it. But if they do come, try to make it Saturday or even Sunday. I hear Friday will be a mess."

"Sunday, then, after church."

As they watched the parade, delicious aromas had been wafting through the house. The unmistakable scent of roasting turkey made Rafe ravenous, but there were still several hours until they would eat dinner.

Mike sent his kids to take a bath and get dressed.

When they returned, they wore what Rafe called "Sunday clothes."

Catherine had donned a light blue dress with a lace collar and pulled her hair back with a matching blue band.

Matthew wore khaki pants and struggled to get his shirt buttoned.

Rafe beckoned the boy over. "Here, kid, let me help you. If you always start at the bottom and button up, you won't get them out of order."

Matthew did what he suggested and grinned when it worked. "Okay, Uncle Rafe."

He hadn't paid attention before, but Mike wore khaki pants and a jade green shirt.

Charlotte came to clear and set the dining room table wearing black slacks and a multicolored sweater. Rafe began to feel underdressed in his faded jeans and old sports team T-shirt. "Is everyone dressing up for dinner?"

"Yeah, we usually do. But you're fine. You don't have to change."

Rafe considered it for about two minutes. He figured Gabe and his bunch would arrive dressed spiffy, too. Probably Sheena and her grandmother would also dress for the occasion. He decided to put on less ragged jeans and the Henley he'd bought at the mall. "I think I will, though. I don't want to be the only one looking like a slob."

Matthew tagged along when Rafe headed over to his apartment to change. The kids had visited his place once or twice but now, as Rafe changed, Matthew roamed the place. He asked a dozen questions and came to a halt before the one picture of Rafe on display. The standard new United States Marine Corps portrait showed a serious Rafe, face unmarred.

"Is this you?"

Rafe's stomach twisted into a knot. He should have

put the picture away a long time ago, and he had no idea why he had left it out. *Maybe to remind myself I wasn't always ugly as homemade sin.* He schooled his voice to sound calm. "Yeah, it's me. It was a long time ago."

His nephew poked one small finger against the glass. "You were handsome."

He used the past tense, and Rafe noted it. "I was, once upon a time. Let's go back to the house." Rafe wanted to end the conversation before Matthew compared him to some monster or freak. His pleasant mood threatened to evaporate, and if it wouldn't make a major scene, he might consider bowing out of dinner. But it would upset his mom and Sheena, too.

"You were really young, Uncle Rafe."

He had been, unscarred and so innocent, a green Marine. "I was eighteen."

Matthew continued with another comment." You look different now."

And I know it every time I chance a glance in the mirror or see the horror on someone's face. "I suppose I do."

His nephew nodded. "I like the way you look now better."

The short sentence stunned Rafe. "Why? I'm ugly now." It probably wasn't the thing to say to a kid, but it slipped out.

Matthew shook his head with a vigorous motion. "No, no, you're different, but it's the way you are. I'm used to it, and I wouldn't have recognized you from the picture."

Overcome with emotion, thanks to the wise words of a little boy, Rafe's throat choked shut with unshed tears. To cover it and because he wouldn't know what to say if he could speak, he picked up Matthew, as big as he was, and gave him a tight bear hug. Then he carried him down the stairs, across the yard, and into the house.

Mom glanced up as they entered the kitchen and frowned. "Rafe? What in the world?"

He put Matthew down and ignored her question. "How long is it until dinner?"

"We'll eat at two. It's just eleven thirty."

"Okay." Rafe put on a bright tone. He could eat now, and he longed to see Sheena.

Mom offered him a knowing smile. "Sheena called, by the way."

She's not coming after all. It figures. Disappointment flared, but he tried not to let it show. "Did she?"

His mother shot him an inquisitive look. "Yes, she did. She wanted to talk to you but since you weren't here, she left a message."

Rafe steeled himself not to show hurt when he heard whatever reason she wouldn't be joining them. "What was it?"

"She wanted to know if you would pick her and Gretchen up, if you didn't mind. Her car has a flat tire."

"So, she's still coming to dinner?" Relief swamped him so much he leaned against the counter for support.

Anne narrowed her eyes and sent a concerned glance his direction. "Yes, of course. Rafe, is everything all right?"

His lips stretched into a grin. "It's all good, now. What time should I pick them up?"

"Sheena said noon."

It was close enough now. "I'll go. Maybe I can change the tire for her."

His mom beamed at him. "That would be a kind thing to do, Rafe."

He pulled the keys from his pocket.

Matthew tugged his hand. "Can I come, too?"

Pleased his nephew wanted to tag along, Rafe grinned. "Ask your mom or dad. If they don't mind, then you can." With Matthew in tow, Rafe headed for Sheena's house. He noticed the flat as soon as he pulled up behind her car. When he rang the doorbell, he saw the door open so fast she must have been waiting.

"Hi. I hope it's not too much trouble to give us a ride."

It wasn't. He was glad to do it. "No, it's fine. You look pretty." As he expected, she wore a dress, a shirtwaist style, deep green with a pattern of black flowers scattered across it.

"Thanks, Rafe. I appreciate this. Hi, Matthew."

He had forgotten she would know the kid. "Do you have a good spare tire?"

"I do. It's in the trunk."

"I'm going to change it for you now. You're still riding with me, but it'll be fixed for tomorrow."

Her cheeks pinked. "You don't have to go to so much trouble," she protested.

"I don't mind but I'd rather do it now than after dinner," he told her and gave her a smile. "I won't want to do anything once I'm full."

Thirty minutes later, right on schedule, with Matthew riding shotgun with Sheena and her grandmother in the back seat, Rafe brought the ladies to the house. He carried in the box with two pies, one pumpkin and one pecan. In his absence, his mom had dressed for dinner, too.

Gabe's family arrived soon after. Amber carried Sean, the youngest, a toddler just recently walking, as the other two kids ran into the house with excitement. Eamon and Matthew teamed up. Before long, the boys had set up a toy race car track on the stair landing and were occupied with their cars.

Deirdre, almost two years older than when his appearance frightened her, eyed him, but she didn't cry.

With the women clustered in the kitchen, the three brothers hung out and talked.

Uncle Wade and Aunt Rose arrived with his grandmother, Ruth.

Two more sets of aunts and uncles showed up along with two or three grown cousins. Two brought spouses, and one couple brought along their seven-year-old child.

When dinner was served, the adults shared the dining room table while the kids were seated at a smaller table Rafe remembered from his own childhood. Everything tasted wonderful, from the turkey and sage dressing to the sweet potatoes and the pies. The conversation never lagged, and as far as he could tell, no one stared at his mangled face. His grandmother kissed him on the cheek, the scarred one, without any visible signs it upset her. Rafe relaxed, with Sheena seated beside him, and enjoyed the family gathering more than he had in years.

Afterward, once the dishes were done with the women washing and the men drying and putting things away, one group played board games on the dining room table.

Mom, Grandma Ruth, and some of the aunts sat in the kitchen, reminiscing about old times.

The kids, bursting with energy despite the huge meal, ran around in the backyard until one by one they crashed for naps.

Gretchen joined Mom's bunch, but Sheena remained with Rafe.

He and his brothers sprawled around the living room. A football game played on the television, but half dozing and somnolent, no one paid much attention to it.

When Uncle Wade left, he took Gretchen home.

Sheena opted to stay. She made no move to rise from the couch or pick up her purse. "Rafe can drop me off later."

He nodded.

By the time dark fell, everyone had headed for home except Sheena. She sat beside Rafe on the couch.

He couldn't remember the last time he had been this boneless or relaxed or full. He groaned. It wouldn't seem like Thanksgiving if he didn't have a little stomachache. "I ate too much."

Sheena laughed as she rubbed her tummy. "I think everyone did."

As far as he was concerned, she could stay until midnight but he had to ask. "What time do you want to go home?"

She curled her fingers around his. "Are you trying to run me off?"

"No way. I like having you here. Besides, I wanted to show you my humble digs before you leave."

"Then show me. We both work tomorrow, and it's going to be a crazy day. I have to be there early—the bookstore is opening at seven with Black Friday specials. Do you work your regular shift?"

Rafe stretched. "Yeah, I do." He rose, took her hand, and led her up to his apartment over the garage. Her presence filled up the empty space, and as she stood, hands on hips, studying the place, Rafe almost kissed her again. "Here it is, home sweet home. It's not much, I know."

"There's nothing wrong with this place. It's simple, and besides, it's not like you plan to stay here forever."

Funny thing is, until recently, he had. Rafe hadn't bothered to envision a life other than what he'd lived since his return. "I guess not."

Sheena peeked into his bedroom and then returned to sit on his rump sprung couch.

"Come sit down for a minute," she said, patting the cushion beside her. "I don't think you got much rest, even with a day off."

Rafe shrugged. "It's no big deal."

"You might think so after the holiday shoppers swarm the mall, half of them with kids who want to sit on Santa's lap if you're already exhausted."

He nodded and sat. "Right now, all I want is to take off my shoes and lay down for a while."

"Go ahead."

"I will, after I drive you home."

She pouted, a little.

Rafe laughed. "I'm not trying to get rid of you, I promise."

"Then get comfortable, just for a little bit."

He shouldn't and knew it. But the temptation was too great, so he kicked off his shoes. With Sheena seated on the end, there wasn't room to stretch out on the couch, but after a few moments, he did.

She patted her knees. "You can put your head in my lap."

If he hadn't been so tired, so full that his stomach still ached a little, and so into her, he would have had the sense to say "no." But the idea appealed so much that he did, ending up with his scarred side resting against her knees. "Just for a few minutes."

Sheena nodded.

But her fingers stroked the hair back from his face with such gentle movements, it made him sleepy. Her tenderness surprised and pleased him, and he struggled to stay awake to savor the experience. Rafe failed. He drifted asleep and never awakened until Mike knocked at the door, calling their names.

Once Rafe had roused, he gestured his head toward the door. "Go ahead and answer it. It's my brother."

Mike's had a worry line wrinkling his forehead. "It's after ten, and Gretchen called wondering when Sheena would be home."

"I'm sorry, brother." Rafe ran a hand through his hair and yawned. "I guess I fell asleep."

Mike's expression shifted from irritated concern to speculation, but he shrugged. "All right, no harm done. Take her home, though. It's late."

They said little on the way although Rafe thought they were in accord.

At her grandmother's house, she brushed her lips across his in a swift kiss before saying good-night.

Once home, he slept little, wondering about Sheena and whether Black Friday would be as rough as he thought.

Chapter Eight

For the first time since being medevaced out of Afghanistan, spending many long months in a series of medical facilities, and struggling to adapt to civilian life, Rafe relaxed his guard. He reported for work on Black Friday in high spirits. Despite the incredible number of vehicles filling the mall parking lots and the heavier-than-usual traffic en route, he remained in a good mood. As he donned his padding and the red suit, he hummed "Jingle Bells" and would have whistled if his permanently drooping lip didn't make it impossible. When Rafe emerged from the employee break room area, he was met by the mall manager before he reached the mall. "Hi, Steve." He'd met him no more than a few times since his employment, but he liked the man. Like him, he'd been polished by the USMC.

Steve nodded. "So, how's the Santa gig going for you?"

"Better than I expected." Rafe was curious why he asked, now.

Steve met his gaze. "Today's going to be rough. The crowds are already crazy out there. We've got extra security in place, but even so, we've had three shopper fights over sale merchandise. This will be, without doubt, the worst day of the season for you. Parents are overeager, kids are excited, and the competition is fierce. Are you ready for this?"

Rafe thought he was. "I sure hope so."

Steve slapped him on the back. "So do I, Rafe, so do I."

Rafe expected the day to be hectic and chaotic. Numerous kids would climb on his lap and whisper to him what they wanted on Christmas morning. Surely they would be on their best behavior with Santa. The parents or grandparents would smile and take pictures. Some would pay for the shots featuring the kid with him. He would be thirsty, probably a little tired, and frazzled, but the time would speed past and be over. Even though he hadn't made any plans with Sheena, he figured he would see her. Maybe they would share a meal or just talk.

He proved to be wrong on all counts. The kids were wired, and a lot of them acted downright grumpy. Half of them came to him with running noses and sneezed all over him. Some of them whined and griped. More kids than usual burst into tears for no apparent reason. Several screamed with sheer terror, as if they were in the clutches of a serial killer rather than Santa Claus. By noon, Rafe had a headache of giant proportions. When break time arrived, later than usual at three, his head pounded, and he craved a nap more than all the cranky kids in the mall probably did.

As Sheena had foretold, the mall had become a vivid, bright, colorful Christmas wonderland. Animated displays featuring elves and snowmen took up space down the thoroughfares. Tinsel and glitter and strings of lights were everywhere. Canned holiday music blared over the loudspeakers. So many shoppers crowded into the mall that every thoroughfare was thronged. Multiple conversations combined into a big babble of sound, overwhelming his senses.

As he moved through the masses of people, Rafe breathed in the aroma of too much perfume, heavy aftershave, a hint of illegal marijuana, and a few rank whiffs of nasty body odor. His already bad headache intensified, and any hunger he'd had vanished. Rafe dodged shoppers as he made his way through the bookstore and into Sheena's tiny office.

Once there, he pulled off the hat, the wig, and the beard, desperate for air. On top of everything else, he was roasting inside the heavy costume. Rafe rubbed his temples and willed the pain to go away.

Sheena came into her office and took one long look at him. She reached into the mini fridge behind her desk and handed him a lemon-lime soda.

Rafe grasped it like a lifeline. He opened it, took a long swig, and rooted through his pockets for some ibuprofen. His hands trembled enough that he had trouble twisting the bottle open.

"Let me." Sheena took the container and tapped out several pain relievers. "I don't have to ask if you're having a bad day."

Bad did not begin to describe how horrible it had been. His senses were maxed out, and Rafe wanted to bolt. "It's worse than I ever imagined out there."

She nodded. "It's awful for anyone, but the crowds and so many people must trigger some PTSD."

"I'm on sensory overload, and all of this is just too much. Not to mention I have a killer headache. I don't think I can go back out there, Sheena, not today."

"Then don't." She spoke with empathy.

Rafe pressed both hands over his face for a long moment. "I don't want to lose another job. I can't get fired. This is my last chance to settle back into civilian life. If I can't do this, I'll have to forget any hope of attending the police academy or becoming a law enforcement officer." Until he said it, he hadn't realized that he had made up his mind to do it or how much he wanted it to happen.

Sheena made a small tsk-tsk sound. "I didn't say you should quit the job. But maybe you should cut your shift short and get out of here. Then come back fresh tomorrow."

Rafe wished that were possible. "I'd like nothing better, but I don't see how I can."

Sheena worked her lips together in concentration for a few moments. "I've worked at this mall for six years now. I can't remember a Christmas season when Santa didn't miss at least part of a shift. They put out a sign stating Santa had to return to the North Pole or had an emergency with the reindeer and he'll be back tomorrow."

Hope that he might get out of the holiday bedlam rose. "Are you serious?"

"Of course, I am. Do you want to call Steve Kristoff, or do you want me to do it?"

Sitting in the quiet office, away from all the sound and fury of the season, Rafe had calmed down a little. "I need to get back out there in a few minutes."

She shook her head. "I think you really need a little time away from all this. Let me call him, and then I'll get out of here, too. I have enough staff working today that I can leave whenever I like. We'll go someplace empty and quiet. Okay?"

He yearned to leave, but he didn't want to cause any trouble. "Sheena, I don't know."

"I do." She picked up the phone.

Rafe half-listened to what she said.

After a few minutes, she hung up. "You're clear. Steve said take the rest of today off, no problem."

Surprise washed over him but maybe he should have expected it, after Steve talked to him earlier. "You're kidding, right?"

"No, I'm not. Actually, he told me he expected today would be difficult for you. He was a jarhead too. I hear he did his time in Helmand Province."

It took a little time to sink into Rafe's stubborn head. "Yeah, I know. So, I'm done for the day?"

Sheena kissed his forehead. "You are, honey."

Honey. It marked the second time she'd used the endearment, and he liked it. *Maybe she uses it with everyone, though.* Rafe doubted it because he'd never heard her say it to anyone else.

"Tell me what you need so we can leave," Sheena told him.

Nothing ever sounded more welcome. "Are you going with me?"

She nodded. "I said I would."

He realized he'd need to shed the suit first. "I need my clothes."

"Consider it done. Do you want something to eat?"

The idea of food made him shudder. "No, thanks, not right now. I just need to get out of here."

Rafe retrieved his clothes and changed out of the Santa suit. "I'm ready to leave," he told her.

"Let's go."

Sheena led him to the parking lot, not to his car but to hers. Rafe almost protested but then decided that although he could drive, he remained more than a little shaky. Besides, she knew where they were headed, and he didn't.

She pulled out into the Friday bumper-to-bumper traffic rush.

"I don't want to go home right now, Sheena," Rafe told her. Home was the last place he wanted to go.

"Good, because we're not heading there." Her tone was serene.

That relieved him, but Rafe wasn't up to any company but hers or crowds anywhere. "As much as I like your grandmother, I don't want to go there, either."

Sheena put a CD in the stereo, quiet and classical that soothed rather than roused. "Good."

Her utter calm soothed him. "I'm not up for a restaurant or a movie or anything."

She reached over and touched his hand. "I know, Rafe. Just relax and trust me."

The single word "trust" shattered him. At the root of his many issues lay a lack of trust. When he emerged from the Marines and was released from the last hospital, Rafe realized now he'd lost the ability to have trust in anyone. He had no confidence in himself or those around him. He'd come to expect people to react to his disfigurement with horror and pity. His family had offered unconditional support when he got home and gave him plenty of love, but Rafe had held back from relying on them. His long absence from church had come from shaky faith. The unexpected epiphany from one of the loveliest women he'd ever known struck him straight in the heart with the force of a bullet. "I'm trying," he said in a ragged voice.

She shifted her attention from the road to him, eyes wide. "Rafe?"

The concern in her voice undid him. Tears knotted into a ball in his chest and filled up his throat. He made no reply. Right then, he couldn't. He held his emotions in check as she navigated away from town, out of range of the harsh lights and the people. Silent tears blinded his eyes so until she came to a stop, he had no notion where they had been headed. Rafe scrubbed the tears from his face and stared.

They were at the river, at a public access point where it made a curve away from town. Within the closed car, he could hear the sweep of the water as it flowed onward. Rafe knew the spot. A long time ago, he'd fished here with his dad and brothers. Although it was late afternoon, no one else frequented the spot. Everyone else shopped or decorated or watched football or recovered from their Thanksgiving feast.

"Rafe, is this all right? If it's not, we can…"

His breath came easier, and the tightness of his chest eased. So had his headache, leaving no more than a dull pain. "No, it's perfect. I need this space and solitude." Somehow, he managed to speak without weeping.

"You're crying. What's wrong?"

"It's more what's right." Then he yielded to the sobs he'd held within. At first, he wept alone, but Sheena managed to unbuckle her seat belt and take him into her arms.

She let him vent, sometimes whispering a word or two of comfort. Sometimes, she patted his back or held him, tight and safe.

When he finished, he dubbed himself a fool but he didn't say so aloud.

Sheena handed him some tissues. "I've got some

wipes, too, if you need them."

Rafe had so much he wanted to express but he lacked the right words, and he couldn't find them, not here or now, but he had to try. "Thank you."

"You're welcome, Rafe."

"Sheena, I'm a broken man. Let me say all of it, please. I'm a mess, inside and out. The outside can't be fixed, but maybe I can do something about the rest. I'm sorry I cried..." Her hands were gentle as she touched his ruined cheek.

"You shouldn't be."

He bowed his head. "It makes me not much of a man, Sheena."

"You're more of a man because you can weep."

Rafe doubted it, but he heard her words. When he looked up, he saw her eyes were charged with fire. Maybe later he would ponder them more. For now, though, he wanted to finish what he had begun to say. "Whether or not it's true, the tears are because you've made me realize I lost both trust and truth somewhere along the way. I gave up faith, too. Now I want to change, to trust you, my family, and the Lord. I want to be a better person, because of you. You treat me like the man I'd like to be, Sheena, and it means more than I know how to say."

Tears shimmered in her eyes. "I see the man you are, Rafe Sullivan. I've been praying you'll see him, too. I think you hid him, but he's there, within, waiting."

Rafe blew air through his lips. "I'd like to believe it, but I don't know."

"You will."

Afterward, they sat in easy silence. The sun dipped

low in the western sky, and temperatures dropped. Rafe spoke first. "I'd like to get out for a few minutes. I need to let the wind blow through my hair and on my face. Do you want to join me?"

Without any hesitation, Sheena pulled the keys from the ignition and grabbed her handbag. "Yes, I would."

Together, they stepped from the car and into the gathering evening shadows.

Rafe inhaled the crisp, cold air the way thirsty men drink water. As the sky lit with flamboyant oranges and the sun appeared to sink into the river's wide bend, he tasted peace. The wind caressed his scars and chilled what remained of his ear. He offered a silent prayer from his heart to God, asking for forgiveness and for strength to find his inner man. Rafe said thanks for his family, for his church, for his job, and for Sheena. Holding hands with Sheena, he leaned closer. "This is exactly what I needed after the mall—water and wind and sky and space." *And you*, but he lacked the courage to say so yet.

"I'm glad, Rafe." Sheena shivered as she spoke.

He hadn't worn a jacket, again. "If you're cold, we can leave."

She hunched her shoulders and laughed a little. "I'm freezing."

So was he, but he wouldn't admit it. "Then let's go." On the way back into town, Rafe watched her face in the glow of the dash. He admired how pretty Sheena was and how much she had enriched his life. She sang along to a Christmas carol on the radio, one of his favorites from long ago, the simple yet poignant "Away In A Manger." Listening, Rafe knew he loved her. He almost said the words, but he held back. Before he did, he wanted—no, needed—to be a whole man, comfortable in his own skin, certain of his place in life.

I love her. The truth of it soared within his heart, and he sang along with her, the familiar words resonating as he cherished the moment.

Chapter Nine

They parted ways at the mall, and Rafe headed home, alone but encouraged. Along the way, he braved a fast-food drive-through window to pick up a small burger and a salad. He had suggested Sheena come over and share a meal, but she refused.

"You need to get some rest, Rafe, so you'll be ready for tomorrow. It'll be busy, but not as bad as today. I'll see you then. If you'd like, we can go to the early service again on Sunday."

He liked the idea, very much. "I would. Can I pick you up?"

Her smile dazzled him. "Yes. If you want to come a little early, I'll have coffee ready."

When he reached home, he parked in his usual spot behind the garage. Although they had spent quite a while at the river, his arrival was earlier than usual so he planned to slip upstairs without alerting his family.

"Rafe?" Mike spoke out of the darkness in the back yard.

He halted. "Yeah, it's me."

His brother approached, face tight. "Are you okay? I've been worried sick ever since I heard you had to leave work early."

He should have phoned but never thought about it. The last thing Rafe wanted was to worry his family. "I'm all right. How did you know I wasn't there?"

Mike sighed. "I went to the mall, trying to find a present for Charlotte, a pearl necklace I saw in one of the sale ads. I went by the Santa Claus scene so I could say hi, and it was closed. I figured you were on break until I saw Steve Kristoff, and he told me you had to leave early. Are you sick or something?"

"No, I'm not." A month ago, even a week ago, Mike's brotherly concern might have made Rafe mad. At least it would have irritated him. Now, he accepted it for what it was and why—his brother and his family cared. "Mike, I got a little freaked out. Too many crowds and people, a lot of sights and sounds, and it got to me. Sheena is the one who asked Steve if I could leave early."

"Are you okay? I was about to go hunting for you, and so was Gabe."

Unshed tears burned in his eyes. Rafe was grateful for their love. "Yeah, I'm good. I've been with Sheena."

Mike exhaled a long, slow breath. He put a shaky hand on Rafe's shoulder. "Thank God. I wish you'd called, though. We were afraid... oh, never mind. You're home safe. It's what matters."

A knot in his stomach formed. "What were you so scared I might be doing?" In the dark, Rafe couldn't see his brother's face, but he picked up on the tension in Mike's voice.

"Gabe and I worried you might have a bad meltdown somewhere, alone, and we didn't want to think about the possibility. Or wonder if you might be so upset that you would do something."

"Like what?" Rafe's emotions threatened to erupt. "Shoot up the mall or take a hostage or what?"

Mike moved closer and put his hand on Rafe's shoulder. "No, nothing as extreme or violent—but we were worried you might take your life."

The words dropped between them like a stone in a well. Rafe shut his eyes as emotional pain washed over him, powerful enough to make his stomach hurt. "I'm sorry you thought it might be possible. I've never actually considered it…well, I take it back. Maybe once or twice…I know it's a huge problem. A lot of vets who served in the Gulf, especially those with PTSD and massive injuries, have committed suicide. But not me, okay?"

Mike grabbed him for a bear hug.

Rafe savored the closeness of his brother's affection.

"Okay, good to know. You're my hero, and I love you, Angel Face," Mike said when he released Rafe.

As soon as Mike spoke the nickname, the one their dad had put an end to long ago, his expression changed as he realized his error.

"Oh, man. I shouldn't have used the old nickname. Rafe, I'm so sorry. I know it's a sore spot now and…"

Rafe laughed. "It's fine, Mike. I probably look more like a singed devil." A few days ago, the nickname would have devastated him. "I can't change how I look, so I'm working on getting used to it."

Mike hugged him again. He started back toward the house and then did an about-face. "Are you working tomorrow? Mom said to tell you we're decorating the tree Sunday evening, if you want to join us, Rafe. Are you going to church Sunday?"

"Yes, I do, and yes, I'm working, I'll help decorate the tree, and I'm taking Sheena to the early service on

Sunday."

"Good deal, Rafe."

He made it through Saturday at the mall without issue, Neither Steve nor his elves mentioned his absence, and the day passed with speed.

Attending church became easier each time he went, and Sunday morning, with Sheena at his side, proved to be the best yet. No one stared, and the majority greeted him with genuine friendship. "I almost don't feel like such a freak here," he whispered to Sheena after the song service.

Her sidelong glance brimmed with joy. "Of course not, because you're not a freak."

Her words carried weight, and he thought support as well. If she thought not, maybe he wasn't. "I don't know how you can say so, but you make me almost believe it."

Sheena gripped his hand in hers. "Then I'll keep trying until you do."

Decorating the tree with his family proved to be fun. Rafe got a kick out of watching the kids hang ornaments. As a kid, Rafe and his brothers had received a special ornament every year so one day they would have their own collection. His mom had continued the tradition with the grandkids. Most of Rafe's were packed away, but when he saw the Semper Fi ornament they had to honor him, he blinked away tears.

At the mall, his comeback from a serious meltdown surprised Rafe. Now, he didn't mind the lavish decorations as much. He noticed Steve, the mall manager, became more visible, and Rafe figured he kept an eye to make sure Santa didn't experience another episode. As the week progressed and time marched closer to Christmas Day, Rafe didn't.

Every day, he managed to spend time with Sheena. Sometimes it was just a short break, but when they could, they shared a meal or some quiet time. On Sunday mornings, they attended early church. Rafe ate a few more meals at Sheena and her grandmother's house. And Sheena came over to his apartment, once to watch a movie and share a pizza.

So far, Rafe hadn't managed to tell her he loved her. The words held such meaning, and he had trouble spitting them out. He also feared rejection. What if she responded by telling him all she sought was friendship? Right now, Rafe doubted he would handle it well. Better not to know than to realize he'd been wrong. A part of him also still believed Sheena—pretty, sweet, intelligent, Sheena—deserved someone better than wounded, damaged Rafe Sullivan.

Despite all that, Rafe enjoyed a quiet level of happiness. He still drew the occasional stare or overheard less-than-thoughtful comments, but he handled it better.

On the seventh week of playing Santa Claus and on the last Saturday before Christmas Eve, the lines waiting to see the old elf were long. Although crowds didn't begin to compare in number to those on Black Friday, a lot of people meandered the mall. Quite a few brought kids to see Santa.

Head Elf Tiffany leaned down after a little girl with braids framing her face stepped down and whispered in Rafe's sound ear, "Just a heads-up but you've got triplets coming next."

"Okay, thanks." He didn't anticipate a problem. Since November, many sets of twins ranging from six-month-old girls to early middle schoolers had sat on his lap. Most fascinated Rafe with their similar appearances. Some matched so closely he would have been hard-pressed to tell them apart. Others had no more resemblance than any other pair of siblings. Some were a little mischievous, and others behaved with perfect manners. Triplets shouldn't be much more of a challenge.

The three little boys, age four, were named Brett, Bart, and Brad. From the moment they leaped onto his lap, two sharing one knee, they babbled with speed. Each one had a mop of blond curls, light blue eyes, and the face of a cherub, but they were ornery. One wanted a big dump truck, another one asked for a spaceship, and the third a racetrack. In between interrupting each other and drowning their brothers' voices out, they fussed non-stop. They wiggled and wobbled on his lap until Rafe thought sure one would topple off. Their antics sent shooting pain down his right leg, but he maintained a calm façade. The harried mother attempted to control them but without success.

"Santa, Santa, Santa Claus," Brett or maybe Bart chanted.

"Are you the real Santa?" Brad asked, tugging at his beard.

Rafe answered the way he'd been instructed. "Yes, I am. Make sure you leave me cookies and milk on Christmas Eve."

"We'll eat all the cookies!" one of the boys cried.

The other two pulled hard at his beard, and the third managed to take off his hat. "Let's not get rowdy, boys," Rafe said with a smothered laugh. They were incorrigible, worse than any of the antics he and his brothers had done. "Other children are waiting for a turn. Are we taking a picture?"

Their mother nodded.

"Let's do it then."

Before he could coax them to sit still long enough for Tiffany to snap a photo, the three young boys attacked him in unison. They jerked off the wig and then the beard, baring Rafe's face, missing ear, and scars.

Rafe went still.

So did the triplets. They stared, eyes wide with surprise, and then at each other.

The two elves, Rafe's assistants, gasped. Neither had seen him without the full costume.

The triplet's mother chastised them. "Look what you've done." She reached for her kids and pulled them from Santa's lap. "Say you're sorry! He probably won't bring any of you a single present after this."

Rafe's keen ears, long tuned to any remark about him, caught the ripple of whispers. He heard the soft comments and managed to keep his expression benign.

Several of the waiting children realized Santa had scars and began to cry.

One little girl sobbed. "Santa's hurt."

"Someone was mean to Santa Claus," a boy he guessed to be about Matthew's age told his mom.

Other kids spoke up with similar sentiments while adults attempted to hush them.

"Looks like he suffered some burns." A woman's voice stated the obvious.

An elderly man who waited with a little girl commented, "I bet he served overseas."

The crowd focused on Rafe. As he gazed out at the

people, he saw Steve Kristoff, arms folded, at the back of the line.

Like the rest, Kristoff appeared to be waiting for Santa's response or for some explanation. Some mall shoppers halted to see what drama might be unfolding.

Sheena came out of the bookstore and maneuvered her way to the front of the crowd. Her worried eyes stood out in a face taut with anxiety.

A few weeks ago, revealing his damage would have destroyed his confidence. The old Rafe would have bolted, creating a scene, and ending his temporary job. Bolstered by recent events, by his family's ongoing support and by Sheena's acceptance, Rafe stood tall. He continued to breathe at an ordinary rate, and as he collected his thoughts, he remained calm.

Rafe reached deep within and found his voice. "No one is perfect. Not even Santa Claus. As long as Santa's been around, it's not surprising he, no, uh, I, have a few scars. So, it's all okay. I see more kids here who came to see me and tell me what they want for Christmas, so let's get back to business."

At first, no one said a single word. Then someone clapped their hands together quietly, and others joined until light applause rippled through the crowd.

Rafe saw a small boy burst from the rear of those gathered and make a run straight for Santa. He recognized him—it was his nephew, Matthew.

Charlotte and Catherine trailed behind, neither moving with enough speed to catch him before he reached Rafe.

The boy crossed into Santa's area, reached his uncle, and stood in front of him, facing the crowd with balled fists.

"You leave him alone. Don't anyone say something bad about him or make fun of him. He's not just Santa…he's my uncle." Matthew whirled and then hugged him around the neck. "I told you I had your six."

Rafe laughed through his tears. He had never seen this fierceness in his nephew. "Yeah, you did."

Steve Kristoff approached. He addressed the crowd. "Santa's taking a short break, but he'll be back in thirty minutes. If you want to wait, it's fine."

The line fell apart as people scattered and regrouped.

Steve faced Rafe. "Well done, gunny," he said, referring to Rafe's rank as gunnery sergeant. "Oorah!"

Humbled and not as horrified as he would have thought he would be, Rafe had one word. "Thanks."

Charlotte and Catherine approached, gave him a quick hug, and retrieved Matthew. "We'll see you at home."

Rafe nodded. His elves had vanished, and the rest of the crowd cleared until only Sheena remained. He opened his arms.

She walked into them. Then she hugged him, tight. "Oh, Rafe. You were magnificent. I was worried when they pulled your stuff off, but you handled it so well."

"I surprised myself." Now since the situation had ended, he thought he might fall apart after all.

She trembled in his embrace. "I'm glad, so, so glad." Her voice broke as she spoke.

Rafe wiped a tear from her cheek with one finger. "Hey, you're not crying, are you?"

Sheena snuffled. "Maybe I am, a little."

He knew she cared, but the depth of her emotion

blew him away and wiped out his defenses. "Why?"

"I don't know. I was concerned you might have a meltdown. And then when you spoke up, I thought I'd burst with pride. Then Matthew—he brought tears to my eyes."

Rafe's pride in his nephew increased. His family loved him, even the kids. "He's a great kid. Come on, I need to put Santa back together."

In the privacy of Sheena's office, Rafe restored the wig and beard and sipped a cold soda. He watched as she blotted her face with tissues. Her tears bothered him. He'd managed to remain calm at a moment he had long dreaded. Judging by her reaction, his unpredictability must be a big concern for Sheena.

When Rafe first saw her pushing through the crowd, he had thought it might be time to tell her how much he loved her. Now he wondered if he even should. He'd come a long way, but he still had issues. With the experience behind him, his emotions were drained, and fatigue settled over him like a blanket. He released a huge sigh. "I wish we could take off early, Sheena."

She sighed and glanced at her watch. "We can't, though."

"I know."

Something in his tone must have caught her attention. "It's not long until all this is over. December twenty-third will be your last day playing Santa. You'll have more time then, to recharge and relax."

He would, but for the first time he realized she wouldn't. Everything would change for them, he thought. These weeks had been an interlude, but her life would continue, she would still manage the bookstore, and Rafe had to make choices about his own life. "Yeah, you're right."

"What time are you picking me up for church?" she asked, her tone unchanged.

He feared she made polite conversation just to avoid any awkward silences. Rafe shook his head. "I don't think I'll go tomorrow," he replied, although he had decided only a moment earlier. "I want to sleep in. What hours are you working at the bookstore?"

Her brief smile didn't touch her eyes. "I have tomorrow off, a rare thing during the holidays. My parents are traveling up from Tulsa for an early Christmas. I thought you might come for supper around seven."

Rafe doubted he could face her folks now. He'd weathered the incident but still had limits. "Maybe." He knew he wouldn't. Everything he'd enjoyed would end soon. It might be best if he retreated now. It seemed odd that she hadn't mentioned her parents' visit earlier. Maybe she didn't want them to meet her scarred friend. He didn't ask because he'd rather not know.

Once home, he knew he should stop at the house, give Matthew another hug for standing up for him, and let the family praise him. But Rafe didn't. He retreated into his apartment and sat for a long time in the darkness, brave enough to let his ruined face be seen in public but still too frightened to risk his heart in private.

Chapter Ten

The weather turned frigid and nasty the week before Christmas. With gray skies and frequent precipitation, it matched Rafe's mood. With each passing day, he became more miserable. Last-minute shoppers made frenzied trips to the mall, and children flocked to visit Santa Claus. Rafe swore half of them had visited him before but had upgraded their wish lists. Although he saw Sheena daily and met her during his lunch break, Rafe said little. He knew his quietness puzzled her, and the distance between them must hurt her feelings. He hadn't asked how her visit with her folks had gone, and she offered no details. Despite his certainty that they would move in different directions after Christmas, Rafe had bought her a present, although now he wasn't sure he would ever give it to her. The ring rested inside its velvet box in his dresser drawer at home and might remain there forever. If he couldn't manage to tell her he loved her, he doubted he could summon up the courage to ask her to be his wife.

On December twentieth, Rafe planned to leave the mall as soon as his shift ended so he could attend the elementary school holiday program. Both Matthew's and Catherine's classes would be participating, and he had promised not to miss it. He took his break early to spend it with Sheena, but he couldn't seem to think of anything to say.

She put down her half-eaten sandwich. "Rafe, what happened?"

He pretended not to have any idea what she talked about. "I don't know. It's been a busy day."

Sheena sighed. "I mean with us. I thought we had a good thing going, but ever since those triplets pulled your hat, hair, and beard off and you stood up before everyone, you're different. I'm proud of what you do and how you're dealing with it, but you're pushing me away. And I don't understand, not at all."

Rafe wrapped up what remained of his lunch. His appetite had vanished. "I don't know if I do myself. I realized then that everything's about to change, and it is what it is."

"I don't know what you mean."

"Then never mind. It's not worth it, anyway." He hadn't meant to sound so bitter, but the words emerged harsh and hard.

"It is," she said. Tears stood in her eyes.

Rafe put down his head.

"Or it was. Tell me."

He owed her something, he thought. Rafe wasn't certain he could find the words to explain his volatile emotions. "I'll try,"

She waited, her eyes intent on his face. "Then do."

Rafe drew a harsh breath, then plunged into his explanation. "Okay. The thing is, standing exposed with my scars and nubbin of an ear on display, I had to face the facts. I'm always gonna look like this. I know it probably doesn't appear like I did but I had a lot of plastic surgery on the Marine Corps' dime, or I'd be even uglier. I know I have to learn to live with my appearance, and I guess I'm getting there."

Her eyes shimmered with tears. "Wouldn't you call that a good thing?"

"Is it?" Rafe asked. "I guess. It's not the issue, though. Playing Santa has been great for me, but it's also been hard. It thrust me out into public again, and I doubt I could have managed it without you. We've had these weeks during the holiday season, and I've enjoyed all the time we spent together. You got me back in church, at least a few times, had me eating out in restaurants, and talking. I've never had anyone in my life like you, which is why…" He almost said the three most important words, but he held back, still afraid.

"What, Rafe?"

He shrugged. "It doesn't matter. Everything changes after Christmas. You'll still manage the bookstore, but I won't be at the mall. If I find another job or try to get into the police academy, everything will be different. We won't take breaks together, and our schedules will probably keep us apart more often than give us the chance to be together. Besides, you deserve someone better, Sheena."

The sentiment that lay behind the rest of it was the notion he wasn't good enough for someone like her.

Tears poured down her cheeks as she strangled a sob. "Oh, this is what it's about. You don't think you're what I want or need. You're still hung up on the idea you lack good looks and other things. Do you think I'm so shallow that I can't realize what's underneath, Rafe? Do you think I judge people by the outside, not what is within?"

Rafe wanted to take her into his arms and hold her. He yearned to comfort her and to tell her the truth—he loved her too much to let her throw away her life on a damaged, dysfunctional Marine. He came to his feet but didn't go to her. Instead, he used sarcasm as a weapon and a shield to hide his own vulnerability. Even as he did, Rafe hated resorting to a tactic he thought he'd moved past forever. "*Beauty and the Beast* is a fairy tale, Sheena," he told her. "It wouldn't work in real life. You don't need a damaged man because you're worth a prince."

Face flushed, she stood. "I don't want a prince. I want a hero. I want you, Rafe Sullivan. Or I did. I thought we were more than friends. I thought—oh, never mind what I thought. It doesn't matter now, I guess."

His heart twisted as he listened, but his feet were rooted in place. "Sheena, please." Rafe wanted it to matter, even though he planned to set her free to find a better man and have a wonderful life.

She moved away and sobbed.

He took two tentative steps toward her, intending to extend his hand.

Sheena faced him. "I'm going home for the day. I don't feel very well anyway, especially not now. I've been so cold since the weather changed, and it's going be to even colder tonight. I'll tell my staff that they'll have to manage without me this afternoon. I'll go make a nice, warm fire in the woodstove, curl up with a blanket, and indulge in a book. Gram is making soup. Tomorrow, I'll be back at work, but you don't need to come over here on your break or anything. If you ever return to your senses, then you'll know where to find me. Go back to work, Rafe."

"Let me explain, sweetheart." The endearment popped from his mouth unbidden. *Ironic, I use it now when she's angry because I want what's best for her.* If a glance could destroy him, hers would have demolished Rafe.

"No!" Her voice cracked as she shouted at him.

Sheena stomped out of the office, leaving Rafe alone, suffering from indigestion and regret. Rafe put on his Santa beard and wig and prepared to leave.

Sheena stopped him with a book in her hands.

"Here's the title you ordered. An invoice and something else are tucked inside."

It was a present for Mom he'd ordered weeks earlier. He ached to say more but couldn't manage to dredge up any words. "Thanks."

Through the long afternoon, everything grated on Rafe. The constant holiday music on the loudspeakers gave him a pounding headache, and his stomach had yet to settle. Every other child whined, and the parents were in a hurry. When he finished at seven, he headed straight for the elementary school. The program had already begun by the time Rafe entered the auditorium. As he searched for an empty seat, he saw Mike waving a program over his head, so he made his way down the aisle.

His brother's arms were crossed, and his expression wasn't merry. "I thought you weren't going to make it."

Nerves on edge and emotions raw, Rafe didn't want to make explanations. "I'm here now."

"Where's Sheena? I thought you might bring her."

His body tensed. Mike never quit. "No."

Mike stared at him. "Did something happen between you?"

Everything they might have had just ended, and his

hopes for a future with her had died. His heart ached, and he thought he might have a meltdown, the first in weeks so he lied. "No, just a hectic day at work."

Anne Sullivan leaned across Charlotte. "Hush, I can't hear the kids singing."

The bright young voices raised in joyful song should have cheered Rafe, but they didn't. All the tunes about reindeer and rooftops and Santa's workshop served to keep his thoughts on his job. He couldn't get Sheena out of his mind or forget how forlorn she had been as she wept. Although Rafe clapped when everyone else did, his mind wandered. His distraction must have been evident because Mike elbowed him when Matthew had a small speaking part and again when Catherine's class sang.

When the program ended and the kids joined the family, Rafe pulled himself out of his misery to congratulate them.

Mike suggested that they all stop for ice cream after the program.

Rafe shook his head. He wasn't up for that or anything but wallowing in his self-inflicted misery. "I'll head on home, then. Awesome program, though. Way to go!"

He fist-bumped Matthew and planted a kiss on top of Catherine's head. Rafe worked his way through the milling crowds. He wanted to talk to Sheena and make amends for hurting her so much. *It's not late, just after nine o'clock. Maybe I'll go by her house and see if she'll listen to me.*

Mike caught up to him as he reached the hallway and headed toward the exit. He came to a stop. If he didn't, Mike would pursue him to the parking lot.

"Rafe, wait!"

"What's the matter?"

Everything, Rafe thought but did his best to fake it. "Why do you think anything's wrong?"

His brother nailed him with an intense stare. "I can tell. Did something happen at work, or did you have a fight with Sheena? Or are you coming down with something?"

Rafe knew he should confess everything, but he wanted to see if he could fix what he'd broken first. "I'm fine."

Mike glared. "I can tell you're not. Talk to me, Rafe."

He shook his head. "She said the same thing."

"Sheena?"

Rafe nodded.

Mike sighed. "If you care about her…"

Care? He loved her with all he had left to give. "I do."

Mike tousled Rafe's hair, the way he'd done when they were kids. "Well, then whatever you did, go fix it."

That was the plan, but Rafe's greatest fear was failure. "I think I should. I just don't know what to say."

Mike patted his back. "I've got faith in you. You'll figure it out."

Once in the car, Rafe put his head down on the steering wheel and offered a silent prayer. His tension eased a little, and he picked up the book she'd handed him. He had ordered the cookbook as a present for his mom weeks earlier. Since he'd paid for it then, Rafe wondered why Sheena mentioned the invoice. Then he remembered she had said there was something else, too.

He flipped open the flyleaf and found an envelope along with the bill, marked *paid*. Rafe's fingers shook as he opened it and pulled out a single sheet of stationery. As he read the few sentences, tears coursed down his cheeks. If any doubt had remained about Sheena's feelings, it vanished as he scanned her message.

Rafe, I love you. You have proven yourself to be an amazing man, one with kindness and courage and faith. I know you think your scars and damage define you, but they don't. I see past them to the man inside and the longer I know you, I don't even see the scars at all. You listen to me more with what's left of your ear than anyone ever has with two sound ones. I believe the Lord brought us together, and I know whatever happens from here, we'll be together. Love, Sheena.

Each word triumphed over his fears, old and new. His heart ached for the pain he'd caused her when he tried to shove her away. Thinking he knew what she wanted and needed better than she did had been arrogant. Rafe brushed the page with his fingertips and then with his lips.

He tucked it back into the book with care and headed for Sheena's house, his heart brimming full of love. Everything would be fine between them, now.

Chapter Eleven

The acrid stench of something burning permeated the car as Rafe drove closer to Sheena's address. It wasn't the sweet, familiar aroma of wood smoke, but something more pungent, and it made his gut clench tight enough to hurt. Although he could handle a leaf-burning fire or one in the hearth, fire still terrified him. Rafe didn't need the ever-present reminder of his scars to remember his severe burns. He rolled down the window and sniffed. The odor appeared to be increasing, and he steeled himself against freaking out. Sheena was his objective, and he had to stay focused, not lose it now.

He drove along the narrow street and rolled to a stop at the curb, up the block from the house.

A handful of people gathered on the sidewalk, heads craning upward and fingers pointing.

Smoke filled his nose, and as Rafe stepped out of the car, he saw a tall column of black smoke ascending into the night sky. It came from the back of the house Sheena shared with her grandmother, and seeing it, he broke into a run. As he got closer, Rafe noticed orange flames bursting from the back porch roof. He remembered the stove there, and his chest constricted tight.

"Rafe, thank God you're here!" a woman called, panic and terror making her voice shrill.

Rafe whirled at the sound of his name and saw Gretchen, in the center of a circle of neighbors. He made his way over. "What happened?"

"I think the flue caught on fire." Tears escaped down her cheeks as she huddled into her thick robe. "We called the fire department, but Sheena didn't want to leave."

A distant wail of emergency sirens became audible as Rafe processed what he'd heard. He searched the crowd for Sheena. When he didn't see her, he asked Gretchen, "Where is she? Where's Sheena?"

Her grandmother wailed and repeated. "She's inside. Rafe, she's in there. She sent me outside but went back to try to put it out. I told her not to, but she did."

Adrenaline and years of military training kicked in as Rafe's Marine instincts took over. He dashed toward the house and then realized he might not be able to access the back porch from the kitchen. Without breaking stride, he changed directions and rounded the side of the house. An old-fashioned gate refused to open when he pushed it, so Rafe vaulted over it and made his way to the rear door. From the back yard, he saw the tremendous amount of smoke belching from the structure and the flames spreading swiftly. "Sheena!"

He didn't expect an answer, and none came. Rafe kicked in the back door and found himself in a smoke-filled mudroom just off the back porch. The sound of the crackling flames surrounded him, and smoke poured into his lungs, choking him. He crouched low and made his way onto the porch. The smoke limited his vision, and the heat of the fire blasted him. His heart pounded until Rafe thought it would burst from his chest, and his eyes streamed with tears from the smoke. Fear remained but he shoved it away. Sheena mattered more than his old terrors. He called her name and listened, but at first, he heard nothing. Then a small sound, a low keening, filtered into his hearing, and Rafe dropped to the floor. He crawled toward it, and his hands bumped into something solid. "Sheena, it's me, Rafe. Talk to me, sweetheart."

"Rafe? Rafe, I can't breathe." Her voice was a harsh croak. She coughed hard.

He managed to get his hands around her. He lifted her in his arms and stumbled through the spreading flames toward the back door. His irritated eyes were blind, but he kept moving, and when cold air rushed across his face, he pushed himself forward. They had made it outside.

Rafe headed for the front lawn, toward help. Her body lay heavy in his arms, and she hadn't spoken any more. Someone opened the gate, and he rushed through it. On the edge of the winter-brown grass on the small front lawn, Rafe toppled to his knees, still clutching Sheena. He put her down and pushed the hair from her face.

She lay still.

He feared she might be dead. "Sheena, please, Sheena." He wept and didn't realize it as he prayed aloud, his tongue tripping over the words as he babbled. Rafe gasped for air. His voice was hoarse from the smoke.

Her body contorted as a coughing fit erupted. Sheena hacked hard and opened her eyes. "What is it?"

He prayed in the frigid night, and when she spoke, relief flooded his senses. "Thank God. Oh, thank you,

Jesus, thank you."

She sat up.

Rafe pulled her onto his lap.

She choked, coughing as he did. "Rafe?"

"It's me." He rocked her in his arms, unwilling to let go. The sirens shrilled closer.

"You walked into the fire for me. You came and found me."

"Hush. I thought I'd lost you, sweetheart. Sheena, I love you. I love you so much."

Despite her condition, she attempted a smile. "I love you, too."

Gretchen loomed over them, wringing her hands together. "Is she all right? Are you okay, Rafe?"

He gazed up at her with a smile. "We're fine." Rafe refused to let go of her until the EMTs were on scene.

The EMTs inserted an oxygen canula in her nose, then loaded her into the ambulance.

Rafe rode with her. At the emergency room, they were separated and treated.

Sheena was transported to a room for a night of observation.

The moment Rafe was cleared, he headed for it. His brothers stood in the hallway.

Both rushed forward to meet him, their arms enclosing him in a group hug.

"What are you doing here?" he asked, although he'd never been so glad to see anyone, ever.

"Gretchen had a neighbor call, so we'd know you went to the hospital with Sheena. Are you all right, Rafe?" Mike asked.

"I am, if Sheena is," he told them. "I'm glad you're

here, but I need to go find her."

Gabe grinned and punched Rafe's shoulder. "We'll wait, kid. You'll need a ride home."

He walked into the dim space, afraid he might wake her if she slept.

But Sheena sat upright in bed, waiting.

Rafe sat on the edge of the hospital bed and took her hand in his.

She clutched it and then pulled him forward into her reach. Sheena kissed his mouth.

He returned the kiss with slow sweetness.

Then she kissed his scarred cheek and planted a single kiss on his ruined ear. "Are you all right? Were you hurt or burned?"

He'd never been better, but her concern touched him. His heart wanted to burst with joy. "No, just a little smoke inhalation, but I'm fine. How are you?"

Despite being in a hospital bed, still wearing oxygen, she flashed him a smile. "I'm good. They wanted to keep me overnight because of the smoke, but I feel perfectly well. I thought I was about to die, Rafe."

His fingers tightened around hers. "Baby, I didn't think I would get you out in time."

"But you did." Her tone was gentle.

It had been close, and Rafe knew it. If he had lost her, he would have lost everything. He had faced his greatest fear and never thought about it. "Yeah, I did. I love you, Sheena, in every way a man can love a woman. I love you so much, and I was too afraid to tell you. I was on my way to tell you tonight."

Her smile brightened the room and his heart. "I love you, too."

"I know," Rafe whispered. "And I learned

something…love endures all things."

This time, her tears came from joy.

****

On Christmas morning, Rafe picked up Sheena and her grandmother at their house. Although the fire had devastated the back porch, the original structure hadn't been damaged. A little smoke had stained the kitchen walls, but a group of people from church had cleaned and repainted them before Sheena came home.

Sheena and Gretchen were guests at his mom's house for the holiday. Rafe kept Sheena close, tucked within the circle of his arm. He could hardly bear to let her out of his sight since the fire. After all the gifts had been unwrapped, he had one more for Sheena. He put the small, gift-wrapped box into her hands. "Open it and then answer the question." He laughed at her perplexed expression and had to smile when her face changed.

Sheena gazed at the diamond and sapphire ring. "It's lovely. If it means what I think, it's yes, honey."

His battle-scarred heart filled with joy. "So, you'll marry me?"

Her eyes never left his face. "Yes, I will."

His family and her grandmother watched as Rafe kissed her to seal the promise.

Their future loomed straight ahead, and he realized he wasn't damaged but blessed. And as he kissed her one more time, Rafe whispered, "Merry Christmas. And for me and mine, we will dwell in the house of the Lord forever."

Sheena's answer came soft, so low that no one else but Rafe heard it as she said, "Amen."

He had come full circle, from whole to damaged,

and back to whole again. His scars would be with him always, there would be times he would struggle, and he might be haunted by his military experiences for the rest of his life. But Rafe Sullivan loved and was loved in return.

Rafe had come home once and for all, forever.

A word about the author...

From an early age, Lee Ann Sontheimer Murphy scribbled stories, inspired by the books she read, the family tales she heard, and even the conversations she overheard at the beauty shop where her grandmother had a weekly standing appointment.

As an author, she has published more than two dozen novels and novellas writing as both Lee Ann Sontheimer Murphy and as Patrice Wayne for historical fiction.

She spent her early career in broadcast radio, interviewing everyone from politicians to major league baseball players, and writing ad copy. In those radio years, she began to write short stories and articles, some of which found publication. In 1994, she married Roy Murphy, and they had three children, all now grown-up. Lee Ann spent a number of years in the newspaper field as both a journalist and editor and was widowed in 2019.

In late 2020, she hung up her editor's hat to return to writing fiction. A native of St. Joseph, Missouri, she lives and works in the rugged, mysterious, and beautiful Missouri Ozarks.

https://leeannsontheimer.blogspot.com/

Thank you for purchasing
this publication of The Wild Rose Press, Inc.

For questions or more information
contact us at
info@thewildrosepress.com.

The Wild Rose Press, Inc.
www.thewildrosepress.com